MW01125900

MAIL ORDER BRIDES OF TRACE HOLLOW

BOOK 1

CJ SAMUELS

Copyright © 2016 CJ Samuels
ALL RIGHTS RESERVED

This book contains material protected under International and Federal Copyright Laws and Treaties. Any unauthorized reprint or use of this material is prohibited. No part of this book may be reproduced or transmitted in any form or by any means, electronic or mechanical, including photocopying, recording, or by any information storage and retrieval system without express written permission from the author.

First Edition 2016

Cover Design: Erin Dameron-Hill Graphics
This cover was the winner of the 2015 Cover The Words cover contest. Thank you, Erin!
Formatted by Enterprise Book Services, LLC

Join CJ's Newsletter

When I decided to write a book, my dad had passed away and my thought was that some family stories needed to be passed on to the descendants of my parents. As I started writing, my characters took on some characteristics of my family. Ellianna and Emma are my great nieces. Elli's eyes do change color with her mood. Emma has fiery red hair. In coming books, you will see Sophia, Maddie, Saralyn, and Aislyn. I will never run out of names because my family is still expanding with each generation.

The townsfolk you're about to read existed in my life. Many have crossed over to Jordan now and I hope that I've captured just a little of their bigger than life personalities.

The entire series of Trace Hollow dedication goes to each and every person in my family. Some are gone now, but their own families are seeing them again through my stories.

Thank you for reading my book. You, my readers, are now a part of my world in Trace Hollow, which is a "holler" in Kentucky near where my parents grew up. Spy Run is too.
CJ Samuels

Thank you,
CJ Samuels

Prologue

March 3, 1892 - Trace Hollow, Montana

Dear Miriam (and Leonard),

I hope this letter finds you in good health and spirit.

You've written many times about the girls in the orphanage in Winchester and asked us to pray for their futures. Don and I have been praying and we believe we may have come up with a solution.

Many men in our town have expressed interest in sending for mail order brides, and we desperately need marriageable women for our town to grow. Don and I believe these men would be good to the girls and feel it's a solution that will benefit everyone!

I know the girls are of age or close to it now. Would you and Leonard be willing to talk to them? These are fine, upstanding, God-fearing men who have discussed their desires for a wife with me, and I'm confident I know them quite well. Miriam, I believe you and I could easily match the couples ourselves. The details can be discussed further if the girls agree to this arrangement. Pray and speak with God to see if He places this on your heart, as He has done on ours.

Love in Christ,
Helen (and Don)

———————

CJ Samuels

April 7, 1892 - Winchester, Ohio

Elli

Dear Helen (and Don),

Praise the Lord! God is good!

We firmly believe you have found the answer to our prayers. We have four women that will be ready within the year. I spoke to Mrs. White, who runs the orphanage, and we agree they should be of age eighteen when they leave here. I will send you descriptions of our girls, then we can match the couples together after praying for each one of them. These girls are good, Christian ladies and have all been properly trained to run a household. Although they're as close as blood sisters, their personalities are nothing alike.

Elli will be the first to come of age. She has thick auburn hair and eyes that change color with her mood. She's a bit headstrong, but we know she'll make a wonderful wife. She's certainly not afraid to take a stand for what is right, and will staunchly defend the less fortunate. Elli's a rule follower, if the rules are fair and just.

It would be easiest if her chosen young man could wire the money for her trip. I believe, though, we should make this a true mail order bride situation and not allow them to learn about each other until they meet—not even each other's names!

Leonard laughs at me for my romantic notions, but I adore the thought that God has given us a hand in young love.

Blessings,

Miriam (and Leonard)

1

Elli Gray stopped outside the kitchen door of the orphanage that was her home, and cringed in embarrassment. On her way back, she'd spotted Mr. Mills coming out of the general store and she'd rushed behind the church to stay out of his sight, only to find his three sons—all around the age of eight to ten years old—cornering one of the younger orphan boys. Elli considered all the children her brothers and sisters, and there was no way a group of heathens was going to hurt a single one of them.

After breaking up the fight, she looked a sorry state. Her torn skirt gaped all the way from her knee to the ground, one ripped sleeve was loosely around her arm, and her auburn hair had come undone from its braid and was now half-covering her face in a tangled mess. She took a deep breath, brushed her hair back with her hands, and stepped inside the door to face Mrs. White.

"Elli, for goodness sake! You're late again! If I counted up all the minutes I've waited on you, I think it would be months. Now get yourself into the—" Mrs. White finally turned from the sink and got a good look at the disheveled girl. She gave a strangled cry and threw her hands up to cover her heart. "Oh, Elli, *no*! Not again."

"It wasn't my fault. I was trying to avoid Mr. Mills and—"

"It doesn't matter right now." Mrs. White sighed. "Get yourself straightened up the best you can. The pastor and his wife are here to see you, and you've kept them waiting long enough as it is." Mrs. White waved her hands. "Hurry now!"

Elli hurried to the wash basin and tried to get as much dirt off her face as possible, then straightened her clothes. She only owned one other dress and it was drying outside on the line. She looked in the mirror and shrugged.

"That's about as good as I'm going to get," she told her image, which stared back at her with a grimace. "Where are the other girls?"

Elli

Elli asked, referring to the three oldest girls she was the closest to.

"Probably upstairs listening at the heating register like they're not supposed to be. Now, move along and don't keep your company waiting another minute!"

Elli walked slowly toward the dining room, thinking of the last time the pastor and his wife had paid her a visit. She had simply stopped some teenage boys from chasing an old cur dog. *Well...their visit* may *have been more because I'd punched one of the boys in the nose.*

Pastor Leonard and Miriam had reminded her that day that she had to learn to control her temper. So, what transgression of hers was the pastor here about this time? She went through all she'd done lately in her head. *It can't be today's fight, they were already here, waiting for me.*

Elli shook her head at the memory of calling old lady Matson a hag. The woman had berated one of the smaller orphans for pressing her nose against the window of her storefront. The beautiful dresses were simply too much for the little girl to resist. I *guess I'll find out shortly.*

She took a deep breath and stepped into the dining room to accept her latest chastising. "Hello, Pastor Leonard. Good evening, Miriam."

"Good evening, Elli." The pastor's wife eyed Elli's tousled appearance with a smile.

"What can I do for you this evening?" Elli bit her tongue to prevent confessing to her outburst in the dress store. More than once, she'd admitted to something she'd done, only to discover the visit pertained to something else entirely.

"Elli, come sit with us and talk. There isn't a thing wrong this time. We simply want to know what your plans are when you leave the orphanage." Miriam stated.

Elli relaxed and took a seat as Mrs. White came in with fresh coffee and filled their cups.

"Elli, we know on your eighteenth birthday you'll have to leave the orphanage. We're concerned about your future. What are you planning to do, dear?" Miriam leaned forward, holding her cup in her hands, while Pastor Leonard and Mrs. White just sat back and listened.

"I'm going to continue working at the diner, and I'll rent a room at the boardinghouse. Sophia, Maddie, and Saralyn all turn eighteen within the next year as well.

The four of us were raised as sisters, and we plan to stay together."

At the sound of muffled whispers, the four of them looked up toward the ceiling. Obviously, the other girls were exactly where Mrs. White thought they'd be, eavesdropping at the heavy metal heating register.

"No one has asked for your hand?" Miriam asked, looking quite serious.

"There is no one here that interests me, and no man wants to consider an orphan for a wife. Our town has grown, and there are too many girls with something valuable to bring to a marriage. I have nothing to offer."

"Now, Elli, Mr. Mills has shown quite the interest in you," Mrs. White interrupted. "He has a nice farm just outside of town and three fine sons to work it. Those boys only need a mother to whip their manners into top shape."

"Mr. Mills is old and he's looking for some poor, obedient woman to cook and manage those brutal boys. I'll not be marrying Mr. Mills, Mrs. White."

"Elli Gray! I'll not have you speaking about a church-going man like Mr. Mills as if he and his family were heathen!" Mrs. White's face flushed with embarrassment at Elli's poor manners.

"Mr. Mills and those boys of his smell and when I first saw the man, his eyebrows were so bushy, I thought he had bangs. I will not marry Mr. Mills, and I pity the poor woman that does!"

Pastor Leonard covered his face with a napkin, but his eyes and audible snort gave his laughter away. Miriam tried to frown, but couldn't quite manage it.

"Elli, we understand your situation. In fact, we have an offer to make. A proposal, I guess I should call it. Mrs. White, could you leave us to talk among ourselves?"

Smoothing her hair, as if it were out of place, with cheeks still pink from embarrassment, the headmistress of the orphanage stood and walked into the kitchen. Miriam waited until she heard the door to the kitchen shut firmly before turning back to Elli.

"Pastor Leonard has a brother named Don in Trace Hollow, Montana. His wife, Helen, and I have written to each other for more than twenty years. They were both raised here in Winchester, but felt the call to go west. Don has been the pastor of a small congregation there all this time, and their town has grown. Helen tells me it's not the 'Wild West' we've all been taught anymore. It's still a lot of work for any woman, but the area they live in is settled." Miriam finished and took a sip of her coffee.

"What has that to do with me?" Elli inquired, scrunching her nose with confusion.

"I'm fairly certain I saw you reading the newspaper while hiding behind the church a few months ago. Have you looked at any of the mail order bride notices that were in there?"

Elli blushed at Miriam's question, though she wasn't sure if she was blushing because of having been caught hiding, or if it were the mention of mail order brides. "I did and decided against it. We may not have blood between us, but my sisters and I need each other very much. We've been raised in this house together almost our entire lives, we're family. We've discussed it and we simply cannot split up. The four of us can manage a home together, if need be."

"Elli, Trace Hollow has many eligible men, many church-going, respectable men, according to Helen, and I trust her explicitly. There's a man who has offered to send the fare for you to travel there. You would still be a mail order bride, but unlike most mail order brides, you will be married to a man with references."

Elli hesitated. Oh, in her heart she longed to say yes immediately. She yearned to be a wife and have a house *full* of children, but she simply couldn't do it.

"Not if it will mean leaving Sophia, Maddie, and Saralyn behind. We've made an agreement to stay together." Elli said, with tears in her eyes.

"Oh, Elli! My dear, I do hope you'll forgive me as I hadn't meant to keep it a secret, but all you girls will turn eighteen within a year, and the others are going to be offered the same opportunity we're giving to you. *All* of you will be living in Trace Hollow eventually!"

The noise upstairs was deafening. The trio downstairs tilted their heads back as one and followed the path as three pairs of shoes pounded from the register, crossed the room, out the door, then down the stairs. Falling through the door of the dining room, all three girls yelled a resounding "*Yes!*"

As they untangled themselves from each other and straightened their skirts, Elli turned to the pastor and his wife. "When would I leave?"

"We already have the money for your train ticket and the stagecoach, which you will use the rest of the way to Trace Hollow once you get off the train. Pastor Leonard can buy the tickets tomorrow if you can be ready to leave in a few days?"

Elli agreed she could be ready and beamed at the couple and her sisters. She could hardly believe it, but in just a few short days, she was headed to Trace Hollow, Montana!

Elli walked Pastor Leonard and Miriam to the entry hall and watched wistfully as he held the door open for his wife, then gently took her hand as they descended the front steps.

I hope one day I will have love like that.

She wiped a tear from her eye, then felt the excitement hit her all over again when she turned and saw her sisters, waiting for her. When she ran to them, the house experienced a level of noise like nothing it had ever heard before. All four girls screamed, cried tears of joy, jumped around, and each one spoke louder and louder, as they made an attempt to be heard. Elli didn't have much time, and there was so much to do!

Finally, the girls decided it was too late to do anything about it that night, and went up the stairs to bed.

Elli could only pray she'd be able to sleep for even a short time.

As they left the orphanage, Miriam told her husband they needed to pray for Elli.

"I think we need to pray for Trace Hollow and Elli's future husband even more. He has no idea what he's getting with our headstrong Elli." Pastor Leonard chuckled and shook his head. He then offered his arm to his wife and placed his hand atop hers where it rested on his forearm. As the moon rose slowly in the sky, and the stars began to twinkle above their heads, the couple, so deeply in love, walked back to the parsonage while discussing what Elli would need for her trip.

The next day, Elli was standing over the bed she'd shared with Sophia for most of her life, adding as much as she could to her carpet bag. None of the girls owned much, but trying to put it all into one crate and one bag was becoming a challenge.

"We don't even own a single traveling dress among us," Sophia said, her voice wobbling as she brushed a tear from her cheek.

"For goodness sake! What does it matter? Elli is beautiful, no matter what. No one has eyes quite like Elli," Maddie said as she stared out the window with a glazed expression and a dreamy tone to her voice. "Gray, blue, brown and green. I've never seen another person with eyes like hers. Her new husband will fall in love right away...as soon as he catches the first glimpse of her! In fact—"

"We only have one day to get her ready," Saralyn interrupted. She had to do that with Maddie sometimes. "There's much to do, so less talk and more doing, ladies! Now, we can make due with what we have for Elli, and just hope and pray people drop more clothes in the orphan's donation box. We have more time to plan for the rest of us." Saralyn had always been the most practical of all four girls.

A knock sounded from below, and Elli headed for the stairs "I'm going to answer the door while the three of you decide if I'll be meeting my new husband with or without clothing." Elli smiled warmly to show she was teasing and left the room.

She walked downstairs and opened the door to find the dressmaker, Mrs. Matson, standing impatiently on the wooden porch with a large bundle in her arms.

"Are you going to let me in or just stand there, child?"

"Pardon me, ma'am! Please do come in. What can we do for you, Mrs. Matson?"

"I've heard of your situation from Pastor Leonard. I've brought a few small things for you. Not from *me*, of course." She sniffed arrogantly. "My daughter insisted you have these for your trip. If not these, she would have donated her own clothes, and I just can't have that."

"Please thank Cissie for me, Mrs. Matson, and thank you as well for bringing them by."

Mrs. Matson had never been nice to any of the orphans. Matter of fact, Elli couldn't remember her being nice to anyone except the banker and a few other business owners that she thought worthy enough.

She sniffed at Elli again and raised her eyebrows. "There will be one more package delivered this afternoon. That one *is* from me and it's for all four of you. Your story has spread quickly, and I think you're better off out in the west. Make sure the other three know Cissie demanded I provide the same for all of you. I would like to have a little more notice on the other girls' departures, however."

The dressmaker turned quickly and hurried down the street. She'd left the front door open so Elli walked over and shut it with a sigh, then gathered the packages and took them upstairs to see what Cissie had sent her.

"You're certainly well-set on clothing now, and every item fits perfectly." Saralyn was correct, even the undergarments fit exactly right. Maddie and Saralyn were doing their best to stuff all of Elli's new things into the already over-stuffed small bag and the notmuch bigger, but very much appreciated, trunk the pastor's wife had given Elli. "What do you think is being delivered this afternoon? I can't imagine anything else you could possibly need!" Maddie exclaimed.

"I don't know, but whatever it is, I think it's here! There's a delivery boy coming up the walk," Elli said as she looked out the window. All four girls went tearing downstairs, but all four slowed and began to primp and calm their breathing as they neared the door. They may act wild at the orphanage, but they didn't want anyone outside their home to know that. Well...except maybe Elli, who didn't care what anyone thought of her, if it meant protecting and defending someone who needed it.

Elli took the box from the boy and thanked him for delivering it. Written clearly on the brown wrapping paper was '*Open upon arrival in Trace Hollow, prior to the wedding ceremony.*'

"What do you think it could be?" Sophia asked.

"I don't know, but I'm following the instructions. Let's finish packing. I have to be ready tomorrow and we have a lot to fit into that small trunk now." Elli reminded them from halfway up the stairs as she hurried back to the bedroom.

2

Early June sun streamed through the window of the sheriff's office as Sheriff Logan James flipped through the latest batch of wanted posters. A movement outside caught his attention, and he looked up from his paperwork in time to spot the town founder's middle-aged daughters, Bobbie and Jan Trace, doing a very bad job of creeping past his building...and he knew exactly why.

The town menace was on the loose again, and they were protecting him.

At six-feet tall, with sharp and intelligent— not to mention, very intimidating—blue eyes, and hands that could draw and fire a gun faster than most can sneeze, Logan didn't fear much. He'd recently stopped a stagecoach robbery outside of town, then returned in time to put an end to an all-out brawl in the saloon, but *Herbie?* Herbie tested his strength and patience more than any other criminal ever could.

Logan twisted his beard as he debated whether to go outside or not. The two women might have an easier time finding Herbie with his help. In fact, Logan walking around the town would almost guarantee the little nuisance would show up. He antagonized Logan every chance he got. Once, he'd even managed to tangle himself into the sheriff's long blond curls. It took the barber hours to get him loose, and by the end of the day, Logan's curls were gone. His ma liked the short haircut, though. She thought he looked like his pa, so Logan just kept it short now.

He grabbed his hat from the hook on the wall and walked back to the cells.

"Zeb," he called to his only prisoner. "I'm going outside for a while. Be back soon."

"Could ya get me a drink while you're out?" The old drunk grinned, revealing two rows of yellow teeth. The man was sober at the moment, but he only had a couple hours left on his short sentence.

"Just tell anyone that comes in I'll be back soon."

"Will do, Sheriff." Zeb lay back down on the uncomfortable cot. "Sheriff? You heard anything on when that wife of yours is coming?"

"Nothing yet. You just keep an eye out. I'm pretty sure Herbie is on the loose again."

"What! He's a bigger problem in town than those idiot drunks you keep having to lock up, Sheriff!"

"*You* are the only idiot drunk I have, Zeb! You *do* know that, don't you? One of these days, you're going to argue with the wrong fence post, and your hands are going to take two weeks to heal."

"Aw, Sheriff. I don't hurt nobody."

"Just yourself."

Logan peered out the door to see if by any chance Herbie had been found yet. No sign of the blasted troublemaker, but now he spied *three* women scuttling from doorway to doorway and sneaking around corners of buildings. The posse had gained a member—the sheriff's own ma, Emma.

Logan sighed and stepped outside. He kept his head down so the women wouldn't know he was aware of them but his eyes, hidden beneath the brim of his hat, saw everything. His traitorous ma ducked behind the mercantile, with a short "Eek!" and skirts flying when she caught sight of him, causing him to fight back a grin, but the Trace women weren't as lucky. Approaching from behind the jail, Jan and Bobbie ran right into Logan as they turned the corner of the building.

Jan screamed, and Bobbie dropped to her knees, covering her head. Slowly, she looked up and found the sheriff gazing down at her with one raised brow and a smirk on his lips. He held his hand down to her, hoisted her to her feet, and she began brushing dirt off her skirts to avoid looking him in the eye...and he knew it.

"Afternoon, ladies. What were you doing back there?"

They looked at each other, faces flushed. "Why, not a thing!" both women exclaimed at the same time. A good clue they were up to no good.

Logan shook his head and sighed. "Where did you last see him?"

"Now, Sheriff!" Bobbie talked fast, her cheeks reddening and her fast-moving arms about to whip up a dust storm. "You know he's harmless. He's just a bit...*spirited* is all."

"That's right, and Herbie looks up to you. Honest! He's a good boy, Sheriff." Jan smiled, as her gaze pleaded with Logan to agree.

"He should be locked up tight for life, and if he keeps all this up, I'll make sure he is. That '*boy*,' as you call him, has been nothing but a troublemaker since the day he was born! Not only has he terrorized other people in this town, but he's attacked *me* more than once, ruined my hat, tore two shirts, and I'm not even bringing up the hair fiasco again!"

"Well, your hair *does* look nice this way. If you recall, I did tell you I liked it," his ma spoke up from behind him. She'd given up hiding, unable to resist butting into the conversation.

"Let's go look," Logan said, sighing as he shook his head.

A half hour later, they still hadn't found him.

"I'm going back to check on Zeb. If Herbie shows up there, I'll let you ladies know."

Jan and Bobbie took each other's hands, hopeful expressions on their faces. "We knew deep down you liked him, Sheriff," Bobbie said.

"Herbie has a good heart and the sheriff knows it," Jan agreed.

"Let's go over to the mercantile and see if George has tea ready, ladies. We can look through the window and watch for him.
Could be he'll show up there and save us all the trouble of searching," Emma said.

Her brother, Logan's uncle, owned the general store. Uncle George kept barrels on the porch for the men to play checkers and tea was always available inside for the ladies. In the winter, he moved stock around and the men were allowed to continue their game inside. It was crowded at times, but it gave everyone a place to visit.

The ladies headed to the store, while looking and calling for Herbie.

Logan went back to the jail, but stopped in his tracks when he looked through the window on his way past. The paperwork from his desk covered the floor and his chair, and yells and cursing came from the direction of Zeb's cell.

Logan knew he'd just found Herbie.

A few minutes later, he'd apprehended Herbie and held him in his arms.

"Honk!" Herbie was content now that he was nuzzled against the sheriff's neck.

"Stupid goose! I ought to cook you with dumplings right now."

"Zeb, I'm taking Herbie back to the Trace place and checking his fence. I'll let you loose as soon as I have him caged."

"Fine with me. I don't want to be anywhere near that beast. He hates me!"

As Logan spun to leave, the door to his office opened to reveal Pastor Don and his wife, Helen. Faces pale, they stepped into the room. "Logan, son, we have a problem," Pastor Don said, his voice as solemn as one of his Sunday prayers.

"Why, you make it sound like a bad thing! This isn't a bad thing at all. Just a tiny little surprise. You know, Logan, a surprise is wonderful, and something you would want to happen again when you look back on it. After it happens. When it's all worked out." Helen spoke fast. She was covering something—the pink tips to her ears gave her away.

"Can this wait until I get Herbie back in his pen?"

"I don't think so, Sheriff. My brother, well, he's been known to be forgetful at times. He forgot to send a telegram to me. Your wife is on her way. She'll be on the stage tomorrow afternoon." Pastor Don shifted his tone to apologetic.

Logan took a deep breath and let it out. "Pastor, let Zeb out. Zeb, your sentence just changed. You're taking the goose back to his pen and be sure to check the fence. I have to find Ma. We thought we had a month or so, and my house isn't near enough ready for a wife."

He found Emma at the mercantile, and she shot into action. Bobbie and Jan gathered the other women in town, while his ma took items off the shelves to purchase for Logan's house.

<hr />

He'd built a new home, with a family in mind, just on the edge of town. Two bedrooms and a loft, with enough space for a garden, and a small barn already in place. So far, he'd been more interested in the barn than the house, and although his ma had pestered him to choose curtain materials and fill his pantry shelves, he hadn't listened. Today, he wished he had.

Brandon, one of his ma's ranch hands, was at the blacksmith's, and Logan had him watch over the town for the rest of the day, with strict orders to sound the church bell if they needed him. He mounted his horse, Sampson, and discussed the situation with him on the way home. Sampson always understood when Logan needed to make decisions.

The crowd outside his home had spilled into the narrow farm road. His jaw dropped. Every woman in town had migrated to his homestead.

"Bring that right in and let's get these shelves filled. Put those pans on the hooks in the kitchen. That quilt goes in the second bedroom, not that one."

"Ma, you can't get all this done in one day."

"Yes, I can. I'm not having it. My new daughter isn't coming home to a house with empty shelves and unmade beds. Don't put that crate there, it goes straight to the kitchen." Emma didn't take a breath between orders. "I've got Faye and Margie sewing curtains—"

"Faye? You let the deacon's wife pick out my curtains?" Logan interrupted her.

"Of course not. We all see what she wears. Margie picked the fabric, and they're sewing together. For a man who didn't manage to do any of this for himself, or his new wife, you seem a little too nit-picky, now."

Logan's cheeks heated and he turned his gaze to the floor. Ma was right. He'd worried about his new wife's arrival, and instead of getting the place ready, he'd tried to busy himself by keeping the town clean. Trace Hollow hadn't seen much crime in months. Even the saloon had been quiet.

Old Zeb was the only criminal he'd picked up in weeks, well, besides Herbie. Logan was young, but well known in the area for not putting up with nonsense in his town.

He'd ridden out to check on the homesteaders, gone through his wanted posters, and had even read a few dime novels in preparation of having a wife. Uncle George had snuck the books to him and there were a few tips on how to sweet talk a woman in them. He also read the Bible, which shared how to treat a wife, but not how to talk to her. If he started talking like King Solomon, telling a woman her nose was like a tower, he would get himself in big trouble. The other books had better ideas on what to say to a woman.

Pa would have told me what I needed to know.

He didn't mention anything in front of Ma. The town had lost twenty-six people when influenza swept through, and Charlie James had been one of them. Not a day went by that Logan didn't miss him, and he knew Ma felt the same way.

"Ma, I thought I had weeks until she got here."

"Well, now we have one day, and unless you're here to clean or sew, I suggest you go see your Uncle George and get some presentable clothes and new boots to get married in. Replace that hat, too. Herbie did a number on it, and for goodness sake, stop twisting your beard! It looks like horns growing out of your chin."

Logan swept his gaze over the mass of women jostling for space in his home. "I'm heading there now."

3

Elli thought the train journey would be the worst part of her trip. The clanking, the noise and the black soot that covered her wore on her nerves. She'd tried holding her handkerchief over her nose—until it, too, turned black.

She was wrong. The stagecoach was worse, *so* much worse. The ride was bumpier, and the dust that stirred up choked her. She sat elbow to elbow with her seatmate, an elderly woman, and the men across from her were too close for her comfort.

"Dear, wake up, you're snoring again." The woman leaned across and shook her husband, once again, to wake him up.

"It's all right, ma'am. He's not bothering me." Elli tried to sound convincing.

"Well, he's bothering *me*. With all the jostling and the dust, the last thing I want is *more* noise," the man opposite Elli said, though he'd done nothing but complain since he'd boarded two stops ago.

Elli held her breath. She'd promised herself this would be a new start. She was going to be more lady-like in both attitude and what she said.

"Besides that, you all stink."

Her manners went right out the stagecoach window.

"*We* stink? I have news for you, *kind sir*. We *all* stink, including you. Traveling with no soap and water has been difficult for everyone. More to the point, you seem to smell worse than any of us. I, for one, am grateful to not be traveling the Oregon Trail. Those people had it much rougher than we do. You might attempt to look for a reason to be thankful today."

The silence in the stagecoach rang louder than when the man had been complaining. It stayed quiet until the stage master called out the next stop. *The last stop before Trace Hollow.* Elli longed to tidy herself up a little and she hoped to find someone selling sandwiches. She didn't want to arrive starving *and* dirty.

Elli

As they stepped from the coach, her seatmate was waiting for her.

The elderly woman took her arm. "My name is Lillian, and my husband, Oliver, and I
are buying you lunch."

Oliver grunted in response.

"You don't have to do that, ma'am." Elli shuffled her feet in the dust and twisted her fingers together. They'd only exchanged pleasantries at the beginning of their ride, and she didn't want the woman to feel she owed her anything because she'd stood up to the man bullying them.

"Nonsense, I should have introduced myself the moment you boarded the stage. I heard your name, and I think I heard the driver say you're heading for Trace Hollow."

"I am."

"Mail order bride, I'm guessing?" Lillian looked inquisitive and Elli felt the heat rise in her face.

"Yes, ma'am."

"I've been to Trace Hollow," Lillian began as she took Elli's arm and led her to a small

29

table selling sandwiches and cookies. "Several times. In fact, I have a few relatives there."

"Are you stopping there this trip?"

"Not to visit this time, just long enough to stretch. Don't you worry though, Elli, you're going to fit right in with the women of Trace Hollow. You've certainly made the right choice in going there." Lillian laughed and picked out her own sandwich and some extra cookies to eat on the way. Once Elli had chosen her own food, Lillian nudged her husband to let him know he could now pay for their purchases.

Elli wanted to ask her about the young men in Trace Hollow, but she was committed and would honor her agreement to wed a man she knew nothing about.

It's certainly tempting to ask, though.

Elli looked at the sky above the mountains one final time before climbing back inside the stagecoach. She hoped her new home had a view like this. She took a deep breath of the clear Montana air and settled back in her seat.

As the stage slowly carried her closer to her destination, she spent a lot of time watching out the window and praying. The next time she stepped off the stagecoach, she would be home.

4

"C'mon, Sampson! We have to hurry." Logan said. He'd planned to keep himself busy that morning and had started off by riding out to check on one of the homesteaders. He'd found the father of the family laid up with a bad leg, so he'd chopped enough wood to last them until he could send someone else to help. "I can't say it was a mistake. They did need the help."

Sampson seemed to shake his head at his master. Then, as if the horse knew they were about to be late for one of the most important moments in the sheriff's life, he sped up, running faster than Logan even knew his old pal was capable of.

Just about the entire town had gathered in front of the general store, milling about and jostling each other. The very large, very *loud* crowd waited nervously for the missing man...their sheriff, and the groom-to-be.

"Where *is* he?" Emma huffed in frustration, and maybe even a bit of worry, as she looked for her son.

"He'll be here," Margie reassured the other woman as she put her hand on Emma's shoulder.

"He'll be here, all right. He knows every single man in town will be sniffing 'round." Faye had a habit of wording things in a way that wasn't quite proper for a deacon's wife, but her words always rang true.

Logan's Uncle George kept watch further down the road for both Logan and the stagecoach, although he sure hoped to see his nephew ride in first.

Elli peered through the window of the stagecoach and caught her first glimpse of her new town. "It looks like a bunch of buildings in the middle of nowhere, but a *beautiful* nowhere."

She'd spent the entire trip watching the changing scenery as the cornfields of Ohio gave way to the mountains of Montana. She'd tried not to think of her groom, but even the spectacular view couldn't remove him from her mind. To avoid disappointment, she'd tried to avoid conjuring images of him in her head. It had made perfect sense for her to do so, but it simply wasn't working. She looked out the dusty, open window and saw a very large crowd waiting for the stagecoach to arrive.

She knew, somewhere in that crowd, her husband was waiting. Elli closed her eyes tight and prayed.

The stage shook to a stop and Elli slowly opened her eyes. She put on a brave face, hoping no one could see how badly her body trembled.

"You go first, Elli," Lillian grabbed Elli's hand and squeezed. "They're all waiting for you."

Elli's eyes grew wide and she swallowed the sudden lump in her throat with a gulp. *All waiting for* me? *Oh, dear!* Deciding there was no turning back now, she leaned over and gave Lillian a hug. The woman had become a good friend on the last leg of the trip. "Thank you for everything, Lillian." She then took one more deep breath and stepped out of the coach. She grasped the hand that was offered to her, and finally set her feet on the ground of her new home.

A man, who could only be Pastor Leonard's brother, smiled at her as he released her hand and welcomed her to Trace Hollow. She scanned her eyes over the rest of the group. An older woman, with a pretty blue handkerchief over her nose to keep the dust out of her face, had her hand on a young man's arm. The dark-haired man clutched a wilting bouquet of flowers in one hand, and wasn't much taller than Elli herself.

Elli felt nothing when she looked at him, no sense of relief or of 'knowing him.' He was attractive enough, she supposed, but she certainly didn't feel any sense of desire toward him. *Maybe it has to grow first. After all, it's not as if I truly know how love works, and I wasn't expecting an immediate attraction, anyway.* Elli would pray and work at it to make both happen if this was her intended.

Pastor Don grabbed Elli's hand again with both of his and introduced himself, then pointed out his wife, Helen. They both had kind, welcoming faces.

The older woman clutching the arm of the young man holding the flowers, suddenly yelled, "I'm the deacon's wife, Faye." Elli couldn't see what she looked like, as she still had her face covered by the handkerchief. "And this is—"

Before she could finish introducing the nervous-looking man, a red-haired, red-faced woman with a huge, tight smile pushed between Faye and the man, and stopped inches from Elli, suddenly appearing hesitant.

"Elli." The way the woman said her name made Elli feel like she had come home after a long trip. "I'm Logan's ma, Emma. I'll be your new mother-in-law, and it's a pure joy to have you here."

"Logan?" It was the first time Elli heard her intended's name. Before either of them could say another word, a shout came from someone in the crowd.

"The sheriff's coming!"

The crowd parted and Elli's breath caught as the most magnificent black horse she'd ever seen burst from the woods behind the general store. The man who rode on the back of the great beast made the vision almost...*magical*. A gun sat holstered at his hip and a bright tin star gleamed on his chest, which appeared to wink at her when the sunlight hit it just right.

He was the most beautiful man Elli had ever seen. *Lord, have mercy on my soul. I need to stop thinking these kinds of thoughts about other men.*

I'm about to be married, for crying out loud! She shook her head as if trying to shake away all thoughts of the lawman now standing in front of her.

"Elli, meet Sheriff Logan James. Your groom." Pastor Don glanced from one to the other, safe in the knowledge his wife and sister-in-law had made their first successful match.

Helen appeared just a little smug and Elli never thought about the man holding the flowers again.

———

Logan had taken a shortcut through the woods and saw the town gathered as soon as he came flying out of the trees. A woman, with dark red hair that shone in the sun, captured his attention most of all. No woman in his town had hair that color. Logan knew he was the last person who would know a thing about ladies' fashion, but he did know none of the women in Trace Hollow would wear a dress so impractical.

What a lovely picture she made in that fancy green dress, though! He wasn't yet close enough to make out many more details, but he didn't have to see her face to know she was beautiful. His heart flipped. It wasn't love, of course, but he sure felt *something* unexpected.

Sampson sped up without being told, and Logan could have sworn the horse was hurrying to his soon-to-be bride's side. The horse then slowed to a trot just before entering the path between the parted crowd, and Logan almost fell off Sampson's back when the big animal appeared to be highstepping and showing off, before finally stopping immediately beside the woman.

Logan slid off his horse's back and gave his horse an incredulous look, but then Pastor Don introduced him to the woman now standing in front of him. Logan heard her name for the first time...and forgot all about his silly horse!

Elli. He thought it was a pretty name to match a very pretty lady, and she was all his.

5

Elli tried her very best to remember all the names that went with the hands she'd shaken and the hugs she'd received. She hoped she hadn't been staring too obviously at the sheriff. His blue eyes were bright and engaging, and he never looked away, instead keeping his gaze steady with hers.

Confidence. That's what it is, she decided.

What color are her eyes? He couldn't stop staring, and couldn't decide on any specific color, as they kept changing every time he blinked!

Before they could speak a word to each other, a group of men led Logan toward the general store, and Elli found herself whisked away to the parsonage by the women.

"The wedding is to take place in just a few short hours, and we need to get you ready."

Emma chewed her lip after she spoke. "You *do* still want to stay and marry Logan, don't you?"

"*Yes!*" Perhaps she answered too quickly, and maybe a little *too* enthusiastically, because the group of women in the room burst into laughter.

The parsonage was plain, and most of the furniture was made of bare wood, except for the beautiful quilts laid across each piece. The house was small. Much smaller than the homes back in Ohio.

It's also more welcoming than any big house in Ohio.

Although she expected the work at Trace Hollow would be hard, the beautiful land and the people would make her life so much easier here. She couldn't wait to share it all with her sisters when they arrived

Then there was Logan. Elli sighed. She could now see the real man in her head and couldn't picture anything else.

"Elli? *Elli?*" Pastor Don's concerned voice cut through Elli's image of Logan like a knife, and his face instantly disappeared from her mind.

Elli blushed at being caught daydreaming and finally answered, "Yes? I'm sorry."

"It's your wedding day, you're allowed to build castles in your head," he told her with an understanding wink, then replaced his hat back on his head. "I'm heading over to the general store to meet with George and Logan. If you need anything, just send someone over. Elli, we're happy you're here."

"Thank you for everything you've done, Pastor Don."

"Thank Helen and Miriam. Their matchmaking idea is what got you here. All Leonard and I did was agree."

Elli turned to smile at Helen and noticed the crowd of women had grown. She could certainly see why Pastor Don wanted to leave.

"Faye and Frannie are drawing you a bath. We just have to decide what you'll wear," Helen told her.

"I have to open a package that I brought. It's wrapped in brown paper and marked 'Open on arrival.' It's in my bag. I promised to do it as soon as I arrived and then we can decide on what I should wear, if that's all right?" Elli's head spun when her question seemed to incite the crowd that had expanded to include even *more* women while her back was turned.

"Of course you can!" Emma answered.

"Your bags are in the parlor," Helen said.

"Which one is it?" Faye yelled as she carried a bucket of water from the stove.

"Perhaps the one wrapped in brown paper that's marked 'Open on arrival,'" Margie told her sarcastically...at least, Elli *thought* her name was Margie.

"While we're asking questions here, what's going on between you and George?" Faye immediately stopped pouring the water and directed her question toward Margie.

Elli looked around the room at all the women and noticed that some stared at Faye with shocked expressions, others looked at Margie with even *more* shocked expressions, a few looked embarrassed by Faye's bluntness, but almost all appeared curious to hear Margie's answer.

Elli—tired from her long trip, and maybe a bit nervous about her quickly approaching wedding—couldn't contain herself and burst out laughing. Margie, who owned the boardinghouse, looked at the floor shyly, and Faye grinned slyly. Elli could tell by her face that the older woman had just learned the answer to her question, a question asked about something that was most likely supposed to remain a secret.

"Now look what you've done," Helen scolded. "Poor Elli isn't going to want to ever come to a ladies meeting."

"I wouldn't miss it!" Elli told the pastor's wife with a grin as she began to open the package. She untied the string and unwrapped the three layers of brown paper, and a chorus of "oohs" filled the cabin.

"A wedding dress," Elli whispered as her eyes filled with tears. It was truly the most beautiful dress she'd ever seen.

The gown was made of ivory, with long sleeves, a corseted back, and ribbons that went from the waist, to just above the ruffle at the hem. The neckline and front of the gown was lined with delicate ivory lace.

There was also a note included inside the box the dress was in.

For Elli, Sophia, Maddie, and Saralyn. All adjustments can be made for temporary use with the ribbons and corsets. Every girl should have lace and ribbons for her wedding. The Matson Family.

Elli turned to the ladies in the room and explained who the Matsons were. "They own the best dressmaking shop in Winchester."

"They certainly must love you girls," Emma said as she looked over the stitching on the dress.

"Yes, well...I'm not sure about that," Elli answered, appearing confused.

Just then, Faye announced her bath was ready and Elli headed for the large washtub. She could hardly believe in just a very short while, she would become Mrs. Sheriff Logan James.

––––––––

Not far away, at the general store which was attached to Logan's uncle's home, the men—Pastor Don, Uncle George, Deacon Jack, and Deacon Stan—had prepared a bath for Logan and gifted him with scratchy new clothes. Every one of the men also saw fit to give him last minute advice on both the wedding, and the marriage afterward.

"Now, Logan, the kiss after the announcement should be quick and sweet, even a peck on the cheek is acceptable if she seems nervous." That was from his pastor.

"That won't work at all. You grab that woman and kiss her! Take charge right from the beginning." Stan certainly wasn't afraid to give advice too.

"Sure, Stan, being a deacon and all, you run your house, *you*—not Faye. We can all see that," Uncle George told him and shook his head in disbelief.

"Well, George, that's still better than you! Your wife's been gone...what, almost fifteen years—and you've been secretly courting Margie for the last year or so. Which, I might add, is a secret to no one. When are you going to step up and ask for that woman's hand?"

"Men! We need to stick together." Jack pressed himself between them.

"Why? We all know you only deliver goods for George to get out of the house and away from Fran—"

"Stop! We are all going to stick together, and I'm not ashamed to say I am terrified of what *my* wife will do if Logan and the rest of us aren't dressed and ready on time. So, enough talking and let's get ready," Pastor Don ordered in that tone of his that seemed to make everyone feel ashamed...even when they hadn't done a darned thing wrong.

Logan had bathed and was now standing in a towel, staring at the stack of clothes the men had brought him to wear.

"I'm not wearing wool trousers. I don't care *what* my mother said."

"They look good, and you'll only be in them a short time," Deacon Stan said, drawing his eyebrows together into a frown while he stared at his own trousers he had yet to put on.

"If *we* have to wear wool trousers, *you're* wearing wool trousers." Uncle George stood firm.

"I agreed to the wool trousers. Your mother was pretty insistent." Pastor Don had his pair of trousers on, and by the odd movements he was making from the waist down, he looked itchy already.

"I'm a grown man, and I can pick out my own clothes. Besides that, Ma wants me married and wants grandchildren. She's not going to stop the wedding over a pair of trousers."

"You're right, Sheriff. She won't delay it, but she did leave instructions for what to do if you refused," Jack said as he headed for the door.

"Where are you going?" Logan called out, with only a slight bit of panic in his voice.

"To get Faye and Frannie. Your ma said if we had any trouble with the new trousers, the white shirt, or even the boots or hat, to go get those two and let them dress you. Now, none of us are crazy about turning them loose on you, but we also aren't crazy enough to have all the women after *us* if you walk into that church in anything other than what they left for you." Jack said as he opened the front door.

Logan's heart rate kicked up a notch. He'd rather face an armed man than the womenfolk of Trace Hollow any day. "Fine! Give me the
trousers. I'll wear it all."

The three men handed over the clothes and added the tie Emma had picked out.

"It will be worth it, son. That's a sweet girl you have there," Pastor Don said. "I'm certain your father would have approved."

Logan nodded his agreement. He missed his pa every single day, but today on his wedding day, he felt the loss more than ever.

He shook off the sadness and focused on the happiness he felt. The image of Elli has been stuck in his head since the moment he spotted her in the crowd. He was lucky to have found such a quiet, beautiful woman and life would never be the same without her. Love would come eventually, he was certain.

The pastor's study was at the front of the church, right off the altar, and the men crowded into the small room. They had entered through the side door of the church and were now waiting for the music to start.

The women walked up to the door of the church together, when suddenly Helen realized they'd be leaving Elli to walk alone up the aisle.

"We can't have that! I wish Logan's pa was here, Charlie would have walked her. He would be so proud of Logan today." Emma sniffed and dabbed at her eyes. "Logan won't know what to say when he sees you."

"I'll get the deacon and he can walk her up the aisle. There. It's settled." Faye looked pleased at the thought.

"I think not." Margie crossed her arms. "George, as Logan's uncle, should walk her *down* the aisle, not up it."

"Well, my Jack has experience. He's walked all our daughters *down* the aisle," said Frannie. "It should be him."

"There's no time to argue, we only have a few minutes. I'll go ask the *men* who would like to do it, if that's all right with you, Elli?" There were entirely too many times Helen felt like she had to be the voice of the reason among the women.

"I think it's a wonderful idea. I've never had a pa, and it would feel good to have a steady arm to hold onto while walking in."

"It really *is* settled, then. I'll go ask…" Helen eyed the other women "…by *myself*." With that, she soon disappeared inside the church.

Honestly, Lord, how can three grown women argue over something like this? It should be a peaceful day for our almost-newlyweds. Helen was deep in thought as she knocked on the door to make sure the men were ready. Pastor Don opened the door, and Helen took a small step inside.

"We're all ready and the music is about to start, but we wondered if one of you would like to walk Elli down—"

She couldn't even get the final words out before George, Stan, and Jack stood and yelled as one. "I will!"

The three men rushed to the door and elbowed one another as they all tried to get through at the same time. Helen even had to jump to get out of their way. She watched them run around the church, arguing and pushing each other, to get to Elli first. All she could do was shake her head.

Pastor Don and Logan laughed at the three men and at the look on Helen's face.

"Maybe they can draw straws?" Logan snickered.

"I've never seen them act like that." Don snorted. "The girl has never had a family. She's an orphan. I fear she doesn't know what she's in for with the people in this town."

"I'll head back out there. I believe we'll let Elli decide." Helen hurried back out the door to stop any fights that were most likely already occurring.

The women were still arguing when the men came running around the corner. None of the three men were doing much volunteering, rather, they were *insisting*. Each man gave reasons why he should be the one, and Elli knew exactly what to do.

"Gentlemen?" Elli spoke gently and kindly as they continued to argue.

"Ladies?" She said this a little louder and sighed. The church doors opened and she could hear the chatter among the folks inside as they wondered what was going on.

Elli sighed again. It wasn't ladylike, but she knew how to stop a roomful of orphans from arguing. The ladies had given her a bouquet to carry which she laid on the church steps, then put one finger and a thumb together and raised it to her mouth.

The sound of Elli's whistle pierced through the arguing set of trios, bringing total silence inside *and* outside the church.

With all eyes now on her, she straightened an imaginary wrinkle in her dress like nothing unusual had happened.

"Now then, I believe I have the solution. Uncle George—if I may call you that already—will go on inside the church, and if you would give me away when Pastor Don asks, I would be forever grateful."

Uncle George gave a wide-eyed nod.

"As for you two, Deacon Stan and Deacon Jack, I feel a little nervous. I wouldn't want to get the vapors going down the aisle, now would I? I have an arm for each of you to hold and walk me down the aisle, if you would be so gracious as to hold me up?"

"What about your flowers?" The deacons were simultaneous. They weren't worried about the bouquet, as much as neither wanted to give up an arm.

"Emma, would you find a girl to carry them for me? Then check my dress and hair for me before you get seated?"

"That's 'Ma' to you, Elli. You're going to fit right in here."

6

Just before the music started, a loud whistle echoed through the church and into the room where Logan stood. He tensed, but heard nothing else, so assumed one of the mothers had more than enough of the children acting up.

"Probably the Martin boys again. Little Kaitlin leads those boys into more trouble than their ma will ever admit." Both Pastor Don and Logan had been near a few of the disasters, and Kaitlin always managed to keep her dress clean, though usually the ringleader, while her bedraggled brothers had broken bones and holes in their trousers.

The music started.

"Logan, this is it." Pastor Don smiled. "Are you ready?"

Logan took a breath and said in his deep voice, "Yes."

The pastor led the way out the side door and to the front of the church.

At the opposite end of the church, George escorted three of the women inside, and was soon seating Faye and Frannie. He started to seat Margie, then thought better of it. *It was time to make it known to all—well, to all who might not already know—that they were courting.* He took her by the arm and brought her to the front with him, seating her on the bride's side, where he too would be sitting. Margie beamed up at him, at the same time her face turned a beautiful shade of crimson.

Logan stood at the front, his back straight as a rod, and resisted the urge to lean against the nearest wall or door frame. Ma and Margie looked ready to burst with pride, although each for very different reasons.

He felt as if hours went by while he waited for the music to start. Then, Elli stepped through the doors of the church and Logan's mouth went dry. He was speechless. The dress she wore was perfect on his wife-to-be. The color of her dress made her eyes shine and her auburn hair to stand out even more.

He wondered how her hair would look loose and around her shoulders.

Elli's eyes filled with tears. It was moments like this when she missed having her own family. She'd agreed to an immediate wedding when she arrived and prayed she was making the right decision.

Someone had placed large bows on the end of each pew, and in the center of the ribbons was a nosegay of flowers that matched the bouquet little Kaitlin carried for her.

Then, she saw her groom at the altar and she was more grateful than ever to have both men holding her up. Even though she had only said it to make peace, she truly did feel almost faint. Her feet forgot how to move for a moment, though her escorts didn't miss a beat, and simply lifted her just a bit off the floor and moved her forward.

My word, he's absolutely stunning! Logan wore a white shirt but wasn't wearing his hat, instead, he gripped it in his hands. His hair was cut short, though not nearly as short as was the fashion in the East, with curls around his ears. He looked as though he'd just stepped out of her dreams.

When she arrived at the altar, the deacons stepped away and Uncle George took her hand, then placed it into Logan's when Pastor Don asked, "Who gives this woman away?"

"I won't give her away, since she's my new niece, and I'd like to keep her, but I'll give her hand to Logan for him to cherish and hold forever."

Everyone chuckled as Uncle George sheepishly kissed her on the cheek.

Logan said his vows first as he held Elli's hand. His deep voice resonated throughout the room, and his gaze never left Elli's.

Elli repeated her own vows in a quiet voice. Earlier, she'd read them over several times at the parsonage for fear of embarrassing her new husband by stuttering or using the wrong word.

After she finished her vows, Pastor Don surprised her by calling forward the blacksmith's son, Jeremiah, who held a small pillow with two gold rings. She hadn't expected rings at all.

"This is Ma's gift to us," Logan whispered to her.

The wedding concluded with Pastor Don pronouncing them man and wife, and the whole church erupted in loud clapping.

Beads of sweat gleamed on Logan's forehead and Elli's face heated with nerves, she'd never kissed a man before. She glanced up at Logan and was mesmerized by the intensity in his eyes, which now held her own captive.

"You may now kiss the bride."

Logan only hesitated for a second, then he decided to listen to every bit of advice he'd previously collected from the *married* men. He grabbed his new wife in his arms and dipped her into the biggest kiss the church had ever seen.

The men began laughing, and the teenage boys, who'd been bored up to that point, elbowed each other and leaned forward to get a better look. The Trace sisters, Bobbie and Jan, tried to look distraught but it didn't work. Instead, they looked as if they were enjoying the show.

Pastor Don cleared his throat. Twice. Uncle George finally tapped Logan's shoulder and it was over. Elli stood up straight, her face more than a little flushed.

The church family clapped again. It seemed the whole town was happy for them, and they would be talking for weeks about that kiss.

Elli looked around the church one last time at her new group of family and friends. She looked through the windows at her new town and thought she saw a rather disheveled man step back from the window, out of sight. She was *positive* she'd just seen a large, white goose.

———

The reception was arranged in the churchyard. The women told her it was a simple potluck, but to Elli, there was nothing simple about it. The tables were spread with every type of food and salad she could have imagined, Meats, vegetable dishes, biscuits, and breads of every kind covered the surfaces.

The most enjoyable part of the entire day, was Logan, who never left her side.

"Let me fix a plate for you, just point out what you'd like." The perfect gentlemen, he also introduced her to every person there and said proudly, "This is my wife, Elli."

She felt like the princess of Trace Hollow.

After everyone had eaten, she told Logan she'd like to track down everyone who'd made something to get her first recipes as a married woman.

They watched the children play games and enjoyed the music. Elli was pleasantly surprised the town had fiddlers and even a harmonica player.

"It's going to take me a year to learn everyone's names."

"I don't think so," Logan laughed. "Everyone here has something memorable about them. You'll remember each of them in no time."

"You'll know all of us ladies soon enough by what we bake. Each of us has our own specialty. Mine happens to be sweet pickles," Frannie spoke so proudly, Elli knew she wouldn't forget her.

"Fill that plate and quit your bragging. Somebody has to feed Zeb, might as well be us." Faye piled another chicken leg on top of an already full plate. "Get him a piece of cake too."

"Is someone sick?" Elli asked.

"No, but he will be when he wakes up in the morning." Logan shook his head. "Zeb tends to drink more than what's necessary for 'medicinal' purposes."

"Do you drink, Logan?" Elli looked at the ground as she spoke.

"Not a drop." Logan placed a hand under her chin to lift her face to look at him.

"Elli, you don't have to be afraid to ask me anything." Elli nodded. He took her hand again. "The party is winding down, are you ready to see your new home?"

"I would love to!" She meant it, at least on one hand. The other hand might start shaking again from nervousness.

Logan assured her she didn't have to help with any cleanup, then took a basket of food the women had prepared for them and put it in the carriage that belonged to Deacon Stan. Emma had the men place the wedding gifts in her own wagon and promised to deliver them on Tuesday when she came to town. The crowd cheered and waved as the newlyweds rode off in the carriage. Logan had promised Deacon Stan they would return it to him the following day.

"If the house isn't set to your liking, you can change anything you'd like to." Logan wanted his new wife to be pleased with her new home.

I'm sure it's fine." She wasn't sure about anything, though, but tried not let her nervousness show. She'd seen some beautiful homes in town, but she'd also seen structures that were little more than shacks during her stagecoach ride.

She soon found she had no reason to be fearful. After a very short ride, Logan drew to a stop outside a home she'd spotted from the road into town.

"Logan, it's beautiful!"

He helped her out of the carriage and they took the porch steps together. She saw two rocking chairs with a small table between them.

He opened the front door and grinned at her before sweeping his wife up in his arms and carrying her inside.

The house was more than Elli had hoped for and the eating table was adorned with fresh flowers. Logan continued to carry her through each room, showing her around. The kitchen boasted a pump at the sink and the large shining stove was a nice surprise. A small window over the sink meant she'd always have a pretty view while washing dishes. The parlor had a little stove of its own for heat, and the living area had real windows too. Elli had noticed some of the homes here didn't have glass windows, only shutters that opened and closed. Elli was thrilled she could see the mountains through the windows.

"Logan, it's perfect!" Elli exclaimed softly.

They stopped short at the last two doors. The bedrooms. He opened both doors to reveal simple wood furniture with beautiful handmade quilts to brighten the spaces. It was obvious which room was theirs, as her carpetbag and trunk were waiting inside.

"Let's walk outside and I'll show you the barn. There's a present out there for you from Ma."

"Well, you're going to have to put me down first so I can change my dress. It's lovely and I would like to keep it that way."

"Can't say I blame you on that." He set her down. "I'll pour us both some of the tea the ladies sent home."

Gratitude filled her as he busied himself while she changed and folded the ivory dress, and placed it into one of the empty bureau drawers. She stepped back in the living area in a green skirt and white shirtwaist.

"The green makes your hair brighter and your eyes stand out even more." Logan wasn't just throwing compliments at his new wife, it was true. He couldn't believe this beauty was now his.

She blushed and took a drink of the tea. They smiled at each other as their eyes met.

After they set the cups down, she walked beside him out to the barn.

Chickens pecked at the ground in the pen beside the path, and happiness bubbled in her chest at the idyllic scene. When she entered the barn, her breath caught. Beside Logan's horse stood a paint horse—the prettiest horse she'd ever seen. Where Sampson had a regal look, this one projected only sweetness. Logan handed her a carrot he'd brought from the house.

"Go ahead, she's all yours."

"What's her name?" Elli asked, as she nuzzled her horse.

"We've been calling her Goldie, but you can name her anything you like."

It only took Elli a moment to decide. "Goldie is perfect. At the orphanage, we had a cook we all loved who taught each of us to bake bread. We couldn't have wanted for a better grandmother figure. She had a horse named Goldie that we all learned to ride on."

"Well," Logan said with a grin, "I was about to ask if you could ride but you just answered my question. I guess Goldie will forever be called Goldie."

Also in the barn was a milking cow and a goat. The chicken pen held a rooster, but there weren't any geese in sight, and her mind flashed back to the mysterious goose in town. She decided she could ask about it later if she saw it again.

Elli nuzzled every animal in the barn before they headed back to the house.

"I'll get our cups and we can sit on the porch," Logan spoke so quickly before rushing off, Elli wondered if he was as nervous as she was.

She stood at the porch rail looking up at the sky when Logan came back out.

"It's beautiful, isn't it?" he asked as he joined her.

"I can't imagine wanting to be anywhere else, Logan. I can't wait until my sisters join me here as mail-order brides."

"I always wanted a bigger family. Tell me about your sisters."

"Each one is different. Sophia is tall and practical, and is the best seamstress of all of us. Saralyn loves animals. Maddie is the prettiest of us all."

"That's not possible, Elli, not possible at all." His eyes never left hers as he said it.

"Logan, that was my first kiss at the altar, I don't know much about…"

"Elli, there aren't many respectable women in the west, and I don't know much more than you do." He hesitated. "We can figure it out together," he said shyly.

She couldn't look at him. "I think we can," Elli said quietly.

Logan scooped his wife up in his arms again, and carried her inside the house, kicking the front door closed with his boot. Elli reached out and shut the bedroom door when they entered the room.

They did figure it out. *Together.*

7

It didn't take long for Elli and Logan to settle into a routine. Since he'd only taken one day off after the wedding, it didn't take long to adjust to his schedule.

Elli got up with Logan in the morning and made breakfast while he fed the animals. She packed his lunch for the day and kissed him goodbye. While she waited for him to return home, she did the daily chores and prepared dinner. His mother had also planted a garden for Logan before she'd arrived, so Elli faithfully pulled the weeds each day.

Sometimes Logan came home early, but some days he didn't get home until after dark. Elli usually waited for him on the porch or he'd find her knitting by lamp light in their parlor. After two weeks, she felt as though she'd lived in Trace Hollow for years.

Everyone felt like family.

Their nights together were Elli's favorite times.

They enjoyed a wonderful life and Elli managed to keep her little flaw—her temper—under control.

She learned to feed the animals, brush the horses out, and clean the stalls. Only one little thing bothered her.

At every meal, Logan would take a bite of his food, chew slowly, and crease his forehead in thought. "Ma does this a little different. You should ask her about the recipe."

The only time that didn't happen was when she made bacon and eggs, which she considered serving at every meal until he figured out that every woman cooks a little differently.

I can't do it, though.

She sighed and looked at the list of chores she had made for herself.

She pulled the small bag of coffee beans out and started measuring them to see how many pots could be made by what was left. Once she filled the kettle for the day, she'd pour the rest of the beans back into the bag to know when she needed to buy more.

A knock on the door startled her from her task. She'd concentrated so hard she hadn't noticed Emma arrive with her cart into the yard and leave it in front of the window.

"Come in! I'm so happy you stopped by. I have coffee ready and some cookies that are just about done."

"Elli, you always make me feel welcome when I stop by unexpectedly. Thank you." Emma hugged her and put the basket she'd brought on the chair beside the table. She glanced at the measured beans on the table, then looked again. "Is this for a new recipe?"

Elli cheeks flamed. "I love coffee. Any time of day, really. At the orphanage, we didn't have it often. When I worked at the diner, the owner allowed us one cup each per day. It was strong and delicious. Sophia would take her cup and give it to me because she didn't love it as much as I did."

"So you're measuring it out to save time when you make it?"

"No, I'm measuring it out to make sure I'm not using too much. I've been making an extra pot after lunchtime, and I don't want to run out. Logan told me he gets paid on the first day of every month. I would never want him to go to work without coffee in the morning." Elli looked at the floor during her confession of how selfish she'd been. The taste of the coffee with the fresh milk from their cow had just been too good to resist.

Emma, on the other hand, was angry and not at her new daughter. "Elli, is that *all* Logan told you about his banking? Just his monthly pay?"

"Well, yes, but I've been measuring everything all month so we don't run out. It's what we did at the orphanage to plan how many times we could make cookies for the children during the month or prepare a birthday cake."

Emma shook her head, but offered Elli a genuine smile.

"I had no idea you were creating all this extra work for yourself. Make your shopping list and I'll take it to your new Uncle George. He can deliver the goods to you...better yet, you're going with me and that's final."

Elli paused, but then took the cookies out of the stove and set them to cool for when she got back. Her mother-in-law stood with her arms crossed and jaw set. Elli knew that look and stance because Emma did it every time she was angry. While she was glad the anger didn't seem to be directed at her, she

CJ Samuels

wondered what Logan had done to cause all this ruckus. She picked up her bag of coins and followed Emma out the door, figuring she'd find out soon enough.

———

Emma took Elli's arm when they arrived and marched into the general store like a soldier, where she began pointing at things the moment they entered. "George, deliver entire bags of coffee, flour, sugar, and anything else she needs," Emma ordered as they walked through, checking every shelf.

"I don't want anything, Ma. Really, I don't. We've been doing just fine."

"Nonsense. Those cupboards will be full this afternoon. George, I'm going to the sheriff's office. If my sweet daughter-in-law doesn't pick out her own soap or anything I have on my own usual list, send her one of everything you have. Oh, and loan me one of those wooden spoons you have on the wall. I'll bring it back, unless I break it."

Elli's widened her eyes as Uncle George nodded.

"Better get busy, Elli. She means it."

Elli sighed and started with the soaps.

———

72

"Logan, are you busy?" Emma asked sweetly as she opened the door to the sheriff's office.

"Just going through the wanted posters. New ones came in yesterday, and you never know which face will show up at the saloon. Happy to see you, Ma." He stood and hugged her.

Emma glanced at the cells to make sure it was empty as her darling son sat down and leaned back in his chair. The sheriff was wellrespected in their town, and she wasn't going to embarrass him by being his ma when others were present, even if he needed her to.

"I brought Elli into town with me. She's over with your uncle picking out a few things you need at home."

"If she'd told me, I would have brought home anything she needed," he said as stood again. He walked to the front window to try to catch a glimpse of his wife.

Thwack! The wooden spoon hit the top of his desk and Logan jumped. "Ma, why do you have that spoon?"

"I brought it for you, you fool! Didn't I tell you to treat that girl right? Sheriff or no sheriff, you will never be too old to be swatted with a spoon from your ma!"

"What did I do?" Logan kept his backside protected as Emma held the spoon high, threatening to whack him. He couldn't think of anything he'd done to deserve his ma's anger.

"Your *wife*, the mother of my grandchildren, was measuring coffee beans when I walked inside your home this morning."

"*What* grandchildren?" The spoon swung in his direction again and he quickly stepped out of reach. "All right, Ma! Grandchildrento-be, then. Elli does a wonderful job at home, always has coffee for me, morning and night. Best cook in town too."

His mother's eyes narrowed.

"Well...I mean...you and she both cook—"

"That girl *is* a better cook than I am, and she knows how to cook with less than I've ever had to deal with. Logan, that girl grew up poor, in an orphanage, no less. She was measuring coffee because she thinks she's being selfish by drinking the only coffee you have in the house until your pay day."

Logan's face said it all—surprise, shame, and sorrow.

"She thought she was drinking *my* coffee?"

"It's not only the coffee, either. Your wife has been measuring flour, sugar, and who knows what else since she's been cooking all those meals for you." Emma put the spoon down and crossed her arms.

"I'll fix it. I'll make sure she has an allowance every month."

"Then I'll make sure she gives you an 'allowance' of cookies each month," Emma snarled and reached for the spoon again.

Logan thought quickly. "I'll make sure I make a standing order with Uncle George every month, including an entire bag of coffee beans—a crate of the stuff if I need to!"

"That's better. You will also explain to her about your finances at the bank."

"Tonight, Ma. I'll do it tonight over supper."

"I knew your pa and I didn't raise a fool. Now, you have a wonderful day and eat every bite of the food Elli sent with you this morning, but save room for the cookies I saw cooling at home. Come over here and give your ma a hug."

As if nothing unusual had just happened, Emma hugged him, straightened her dress, and headed back to the store, taking her weapon—the spoon—with her.

Logan shook his head as he watched his ma enter the general store. Trace Hollow's women had their own way of teaching the men what they needed to know, and weren't afraid to give lessons...*often*. He was glad his wife wasn't a part of it. After work, he'd go home and explain everything to his sweet Elli and all would be right again.

8

Elli thought she'd prepared enough storage space before the wagon pulled up with her delivery, but as soon as she saw it, she knew she hadn't. Deacon Jack and one of the men from Emma's ranch carried everything in, placing the items near to where she would eventually store them. Bushels and crates went straight into the cellar, and Elli's shelves soon were bursting from the overabundant number of packages.

There were two types of tea, several varieties of soap...the list just went on! George had sent bigger sacks of flour than she ever knew existed, and her mouth hung open at the enormous bags of coffee beans—two tenpound bags!

"Emma said to make sure and let George know if this isn't enough coffee." Jack swiped his glistening forehead with the back of his hand. "I think she'll come check, too."

"Enough? I couldn't possibly use this much in just a month's time...probably not even in several months! What am I going to do with it all?"

"You do what the rest of us do with an abundance of anything in this town, share it with someone who doesn't have enough." Jack was matter of fact about it, like it was normal to have plenty of everything you wanted, not just what was necessary. "Besides that, I think Emma was making a point to the sheriff."

Elli wasn't sure what he meant by that, but wasn't going to ask. Instead, she sent a plate of cookies with each of the men and thanked them as they left.

Dinner was ready and the table set when Logan got home. Elli didn't know what had gone on between him and his ma, but she hoped to have a peaceful dinner so she wasn't planning on bringing it up. She worried he might be angry with her for a rift between him and his ma. She had managed to put everything in its place and their home was as neat and clean as ever.

Elli

Logan walked in the door and sniffed the air as he hung up his hat.

"Don't know what that is, but it smells real good, Elli." He gave her a kiss on the cheek.

"I'll start dishing it onto the plates while you wash up," Elli called out as she moved toward the kitchen, feeling a bit less nervous since he didn't seem angry at all.

Once clean and tidy, Logan sat down to a much bigger meal than she normally prepared. He took his wife's hand and thanked the Lord for the food and for her.

When they'd finished eating, Elli stood and began collecting the plates to wash up.

"Go ahead and sit back down, Elli. I'll fill the coffee cups, then I want to talk with you."

Her heart skittered. Maybe he was angry, and just hid it well. She hadn't meant to cause any problems by trying to make sure what they had lasted the entire month.

"Elli," he began as he sat her cup in front of her, "I should have talked to you about this before, but I guess I was thinking like a man and not thinking of your background. My parents started up this town with the Trace family, Uncle George, Margie and her husband, the deacons and their families, and a few others. One day, ask Ma to tell you the story of the trip here from Boston. It wasn't easy for them. Anyhow, when they got here, supplies were scarce but they managed by sharing what they had. In just a few short years, deliveries were coming through regularly, and I'm sure you can imagine what happened once the trains came through the West. Other than deep winter, we get everything we need, pretty much always on time.

"My grandparents on Pa's side owned a shipping company in Boston. A big one. When Pa decided to come west, they provided him enough gold to come here and start a ranch. It was more than he could have spent within the next ten years, even if the ranch hadn't prospered, but it did. They didn't have to touch much of the original money. Pa helped set up the general store, the boardinghouse, and most of the other buildings in town. The Trace sisters' parents built the rest. You don't need to count coffee beans anymore, Elli. If you want something, you get it from the store. If they don't have it, Uncle George will order it. You don't ever have to worry about food shortages and money again."

"I should have asked you."

"No, Elli, I should have told you. I shouldn't have let you worry."

Elli

"Logan, why doesn't the town have your pa's last name?" Elli asked curiously.

"Pa refused. He didn't want me growing up spoiled, but mostly, he didn't have a need to feel more important than anyone else. He always told me we were blessed so much only because God wanted us to make Montana a good place to live. Spy Run is the nearest town to here and it started out like Trace Hollow, but they allowed a business we didn't, and the town image suffered for it."

"A business?"

"A saloon that's nothing like ours."

"How is it different?" Elli inquired, completely innocent of the ways of the West.

Logan looked away embarrassed, but still answered, "They sell women for the men's pleasure, Elli. Ours only serves food and liquor, and we hold town meetings there, sometimes. There are no women in Lucky Lucy's except Lucy herself and she doesn't put up with any nonsense. That woman could have been a sharpshooter. She shoots better than her husband, Sam...maybe better than any man, to be honest."

"I'm glad your family chose to stay here." Elli had a pink tinge to her cheeks, but refused to linger on the thought of the women in the other saloon.

"Spy Run is about to change for the better. They've hired my cousin, Maverick, as the new sheriff. He's on his way here from Wiggieville, Texas. Maverick is Ma's sister's boy. He was a Texas Ranger, so bringing him in was a smart move by Spy Run's council. He'll clean up that town faster than anyone could. Speaking of Spy Run, their bank was robbed two nights ago. I'm deputizing some men and we're taking shifts at night to be on the look-out."

Elli's heart sank.

"Logan, I don't want anyone to get hurt." What she was really thinking was, *Logan, I already think I love you and I can't imagine life without you.* "Just...be careful, please!"

"I'll be fine. Keep my dinner back for me? Be sure to talk to Ma about her recipes too."

Elli nodded, then sighed. She'd miss him when he took his night shift—*if* she managed not to choke him in the meantime.

9

Somewhere in the mountains between Trace Hollow and Spy Run

"Pass me that bottle, you mangy cur."

"You ain't got no right to call names, you bootless lout."

The two brothers, Alvin and Dusty, lay by a fire. They'd argued over Alvin's plan to rob the bank in Spy Run from the moment they set up camp. He scrapped the idea when he realized how many men with guns were guarding the bank. Day and night, they had security. He wasn't willing to work that hard. He stole enough from picking pockets to get them by until his next scheme, and he already had that plan in mind. An unguarded bank nearby

"Where are them boys now?" Alvin tried to stand but couldn't, and fell with a plop on top of Dusty.

"Now, what did ya go and do that for?" Dusty whined as he shoved his brother off him.

"Where are those useless boys, anyway?" Alvin yelled.

Two skinny, dirty young boys soon came running. The boys, Dylan and Codyn, answered together, "Swimming." They couldn't lie about it. They were soaking wet, and both looked very afraid.

"Get ready. You're going to town," Alvin ordered.

"Ma wouldn't like this, Uncle Dusty." Codyn knew what they were being sent to do, and their Uncle Dusty was their only hope. Uncle Alvin was older, and grew crankier all the time.

"Well, your ma ain't here and she ain't coming back, now is she?" Alvin snarled at the boys.

"Alvin, you don't need to keep reminding the boys that they're orphans." Dusty stepped in to defend his nephews.

"Ain't no reason for you to be a lily-liver coward, but ya are," Alvin said with a sneer at Dusty.

Dusty frowned, but nodded to the boys to get ready.

Dylan and Codyn got their clothes and readied themselves to walk to Trace Hollow to complete their unwanted mission.

They certainly didn't want their Uncle Alvin any angrier than he already was.

As soon as the boys were sure their uncles couldn't hear them, they made the walk pleasant by taking turns spelling words they knew out loud. Neither of them had been to school since their ma had passed a year or so previously, but Uncle Dusty reminded them they shouldn't give up what they'd learned and should try to learn as much as they could from the world around them. Their uncle helped Codyn with his arithmetic, and in turn, Codyn helped Dylan.

As they neared the town, they dropped their voices. They just wanted to be done with it all and get back to the campsite. No matter how grouchy Uncle Alvin grew, it was better than helping plan a crime.

"You got your penny, Dylan?"

"Of course, I do. What kind of candy you gonna get?"

"I don't know. Let's go look first."

As they walked up the step to the general store, two older men sat in chairs and a few children were gathered at their feet on the floor of the boardwalk. The boys' steps slowed so they could listen to what appeared to be an enthralling story the men were telling, if the awe in their younger audience's faces were anything to go by.

"Yep, war wasn't for everyone. I spent four years in the service for our country. When I got out, Faye and I headed here to join George, his sister, Emma, and her family." Deacon Stan held every wide-eyed child's attention.

Kaitlyn Martin raised her hand as if she were in school. "Did you ever kill anyone?" she asked, her eyes even wider than the others.

"He probably did," Deacon Jack said, and with a cocky grin added, "He was the cook."

"That's a might better than you! You can't even make an edible biscuit."

The story Deacon Stan had started telling was forgotten as the children watched them spar. Elli walked out of the store and giggled at the look on the children's faces while the deacons argued over who was the better cook, until she spotted two boys she'd never seen before.

"Well, hello there. I don't think we've met."

The boys looked at their bare feet and quietly said, "Hello, ma'am."

Elli knew exactly what these boys felt like. Their clothes were worn and she was certain they didn't own shoes. "Are you new in town or just visiting someone?"

"Our family is camping just outside of town, ma'am."

Elli didn't think the boys were being dishonest, but she also thought they were trying to tell her as little as possible. "Oh, dear. I was hoping you boys could help me today. I'm not feeling well and I could use someone to carry my packages home for me, and maybe help me feed my animals when we get there."

The boys looked at each other and nodded. "We can help you, ma'am."

"That would be wonderful, boys. Let's go in the store, and you can tell me your names.

We'll let George know you're working for me today."

They introduced themselves and she introduced them to Uncle George with a wink. He took one look and knew what she wanted. He sized up both boys while they looked at the candy jars.

"Put their candy on my bill please? I have to pay these fine young men somehow." Elli smiled at them.

"Thank you, ma'am," Codyn said as he nudged Dylan.

"Thank you, ma'am."

"Call me Elli. You're helping me, so you should get rewarded. Remember that." With that, Elli headed home to put some cookies in the stove.

The boys delivered her goods in a cart provided by George, then they fed Elli's animals and cleaned the stalls. They'd just finished brushing her horse when she called them to the house, where she'd prepared a lunch of sandwiches and glasses of milk. A plate of cookies in the center of the table filled the kitchen with the enticing scent of sweet baked goods.

"Ma'am, I mean Elli, can we wash up first?" Dylan spoke first.

Someone has taught these boys manners. She pointed them to the pump to wash up and busied herself making sure everything needed was on the table for them.

The boys cleaned every last crumb from their plates and returned the plates and glasses to the sink.

"We have to leave for home. We still have chores to do there." Neither of them looked happy about heading out, though.

"Well, boys, you've done a fine job today. I have some money for both of you. Also, George sent some clothes for me to send home to my brothers back in Ohio. I know by looking at them they won't fit. I think they'll fit you two, if you'd like to try them on?"

Without further invitation, the boys reached for the pile of clothes before immediately putting on a pair of socks each, and pushing their feet into the new, sturdy shoes. Elli smiled. *Just what all boys should have - warm feet.*

"They're new! Nobody else has worn them. We haven't had new shoes since Ma died." Codyn's excited words tumbled over each other as he spoke.

"Most of the time, I got Codyn's old ones." Dylan's hands shook so much that Elli bent to tie the long brown laces for him.

"Well, who do we have here?" Logan smiled in welcome as he walked in the front door and hung up his hat.

His badge flashed in the light as he turned back to face them, and both boys froze and fell silent.

Elli sent the brothers off with a basket of food and made them promise to come back to help her again. They were oddly quiet compared to the chatterboxes they'd turned into once they arrived at her home. It was also obvious they didn't want to return to their own home.

After supper, Elli made two glasses of cold tea, and she and Logan sat on the porch to watch the sunset.

"I didn't recognize them and they didn't answer when I asked their last names. I'd like to go check on their family." Logan took a sip of tea, then pressed his lips together as though in thought.

"I doubt that would help, Logan. Some families don't want to be found or helped."

He stood and pulled his wife to stand against him. His arms encircled her waist from behind.

"That's a wonderful thing you did today, Mrs. James."

"I hoped you wouldn't mind. Both needed trousers, shirts, socks, and shoes. It was a joy to watch their faces. It felt like Christmas to me."

"Are you ready to go in?"

"I am."

"By the way, I don't know what you put on that chicken tonight, but you should talk to Ma. She uses something different."

Elli sighed and bit her tongue. It grew harder every day to keep her promise to be a dutiful wife. She gathered the glasses and went inside, leaving Logan oblivious to her frustration.

THE BOYS HID their new clothes in some bushes outside camp, as they didn't want their Uncle Alvin to ask where they'd gotten them and explain how close they'd been to the sheriff. They told their uncles they'd checked the bank, and reported the town had men crawling all over it, watching for the bank robbers.

"That little town? I heard they only have one sheriff and whoever he decides to deputize when he needs them." Alvin looked at the boys with suspicion.

"Maybe we should skip this town, Alvin. It's not worth getting hurt, or even worse, getting caught." Dusty had never liked the idea of stealing. He was the reason no one had ever been shot during one of their crimes.

"We ain't skipping this town. I've heard too many times that their bank is full of gold. We didn't get a thing at Spy Run's bank, so this is the one."

The glint in his brother's eyes sent a chill across Dusty's skin. He glanced at his nephews, and their pale faces told a story Dusty didn't want to think about.

He stoked the fire, then turned to tuck the boys in and tell them a story. He couldn't leave this life of crime with Alvin because he had threatened to hurt the boys if Dusty did. Alvin had been the first to arrive after their sister and her husband—the boys' ma and pa—had died within days of each other from an influenza outbreak, so the boys belonged to Alvin in the eyes of the law. Dusty would stick things out for his nephews.

Their Uncle Dusty told them a tale about cowboys and Indians, and the exhausted boys fell into a fitful sleep before Dusty could finish. He then doused the fire and sat staring at another empty bottle of the whiskey that had turned his brother into someone he didn't even know.

Or maybe I never did know him.

10

Elli had made it through two months in Trace Hollow without losing her temper, and although she was proud of herself, she still struggled with her anger at times. The work here was hard, but she had worked hard in Ohio. *If only she felt better...*

I could use Dylan and Codyn this morning. Odd, how I always feel so much better in the afternoon.

As she stooped to gather the last basket of the vegetables from her garden, she drew in a slow breath and ran a hand across her brow, willing the contents of her stomach to stay put. She hadn't felt well for almost a week now and tried to get her outside chores done in the early morning to reduce her time out in the sun.

It didn't help, though, she was sick every single morning.

Although it does get better throughout the day. I suppose I should be grateful.

She left her basket on the porch, and decided before she started cleaning the vegetables for storage, she'd write another letter to her sisters, all still back in Ohio. Sophia wouldn't arrive until November. Still, in just a few short months, the girls would all be together again.

She made herself a cup of coffee and sat down to start the letter. She wrote of the town and the people, but mostly she wrote of life with Logan, asked her sisters to join her in praying that she wouldn't struggle so much to keep her temper. These last two weeks had been so hard to maintain her composure when Logan mentioned his mother's cooking. Once, she'd made her tongue bleed!

Elli adored her mother-in-law and was happy she didn't feel the need to hold it against her. Logan's comments had nothing to do with Emma. Any comparison between his wife and his mother was entirely Logan's doing.

She wrote to the girls about the ladies' meeting held in the room next to the general store every other Thursday. All the women gathered to quilt, drink tea, and gossip. She described the townsfolk, but let them know she had no idea who would be matched with the girls when they arrived. Pastor Don and Helen kept that very quiet, although if the gossip were true, every man in town had knocked on the parsonage door asking to be next. Most of the men were respectable, although a few spent too many hours at the saloon, but Elli placed her faith in the pastors' wives, Helen and Miriam, as they had done well with matching her with Logan.

Elli finished her letter and put it an envelope, then yawned. After glancing at the clock, she shook her head. For such an early hour, it was ridiculous to be so tired already. Still, she could just lay her head down for a brief time on the table. Her mother-in-law was coming by to help her a little later.

She just needed a moment of rest before she got there.

Emma arrived and Elli wasn't on the porch to greet her as she usually was, but she spotted the basket of picked vegetables. Elli *always* had the vegetables cleaned and ready for them to start canning. Fear prickled up Emma's back.

Something's wrong. She didn't bother unloading her wagon, but hurried straight to the door.

Elli was sound asleep with her head on the table, and Emma gently shook her. "Elli, sweetheart, are you all right?"

Elli opened her eyes slowly and didn't bother to answer. One sniff of the cold coffee in front of her sent her running outside.

Emma followed and held the loose strands of hair back as her daughter-in-law finished being sick, then helped her back inside, placing a cool cloth across Elli's forehead. "How long have you been ill?"

"Two weeks or so." Elli's cheeks burned with embarrassment at trying to conceal it. "It always seems to get better in the afternoon, so I didn't want to worry anyone. I was just so tired after being outside."

"The vegetables can wait. We're going to see Doc Matt right now, and this is not up for discussion."

Emma helped a protesting Elli into the wagon.

"I can walk. It's such a short distance."

"Absolutely not. It's too hot and you're tired. We ride today."

Emma stopped in front of the store just long enough to tell the young boy sitting on the steps to go see if the sheriff was in and to send him to the doctor's office.

"I don't want to worry him," Elli told her, a tear rolling down her cheek.

"I don't think he has a thing to worry about, child, but I want him there, just in case."

"In case there really is something terribly wrong with me?" Elli's voice shook a little.

"Unless I miss my guess, none of us have a thing to worry about."

Confusion jumbled Elli's thoughts. She'd believed her mother-in-law loved her, yet she could be dying, and the woman sounded *thrilled* to be going to the doctor.

Logan burst through the doctor's door. "Where is she?" He barely looked at his mother.

"In with Doc Matt. She's going to be fine, Logan. She's overly tired and can't hold her food down. Calm down, and let Matt check her."

Logan paced for the next ten minutes. He had no idea how his mother could be so calm. She just sat there and read a dime novel while his wife was in the doctor's office being checked for any number of things. Worry had led him to twist his beard into the two separate horns his mother hated and his wife giggled at.

After what felt like hours, Doc finally stuck his head out of the examination room's door.

"Sheriff, come on in."

Logan strode in with long steps and found Elli sitting on the table appearing uncomfortable, and he rushed to her side.

"Elli, what's wrong? Sweetheart, whatever it is, I'll do everything in my power to make it better." He held both her hands in his, desperation in his eyes.

"I don't think you'll need to do anything but wait, Sheriff. The way you were pacing out there, you might wear out a few pair of boots before this is over," Matt said, laughing.

"Wait? I'm not waiting! Whatever she needs, Doc, do it now." Logan immediately went into what Elli called his 'Sheriff-form.'

"Elli, do you want to tell him?" The doctor's voice was gentle.

She did want to tell him. She wanted to throw her arms around him and tell him how grateful she was to have such an amazing family...but she couldn't get the words out. "Elli, just say it." Worry creased Logan's forehead. "Whatever it is, we'll get through it together."

"I'm sure you will, because togetherness caused this." Doc Matt could hardly get the words out from laughing so hard at the determined look on the sheriff's face. He'd known Logan since he was a child, and he was thrilled for him "You're going to be a father, Logan. I'd say about early spring."

Silence. Not a word came from Logan now.

Waves of terror ran through Elli, and her vision blurred. They'd talked about having a family, but neither expected a baby so soon. The silence didn't last long, however.

Logan suddenly let out a *whoop* and threw his hat in the hair. He hugged the doctor, then grabbed his wife up in his arms. He started to twirl her, then realized what he was doing. "Elli! I'm sorry, did I hurt you? Did I hurt the baby?" He sat her gently back on the table.

"You aren't hurting anyone, but I think your mother might want to hear the news...although, I think perhaps your yelling and carrying on might have already given it away." Elli struggled to hold her eyes open, nausea still roiling in her gut. *I'm also the happiest person in the world.*

She laid her head contentedly against Logan's chest as Emma stopped in the doorway, a thousand-watt smile on her face. She closed her eyes as if thanking God, and Elli joined her in the silent prayer.

Elli shook her head at her husband over the supper table. "It isn't proper, Logan. You can't just go around announcing it to everyone you meet."

"It might not be proper in Ohio, but you're in Montana now. The women will spread the news if we don't anyway. It's not like anyone that doesn't hear it through them won't be able to tell by looking at you soon."

"Logan, the day we walked out of the office, you went through the street yelling it. Within two days, I'd received a crate full of baby items. Now, two weeks later, the second bedroom is overflowing."

"Well, that just means the whole town loves you and our baby. We will be ready when he," Logan hesitated, "or *she* is born."

It drove her batty that he wouldn't budge an inch. She still didn't feel well, and most of all, he still hadn't told her he loved her.

Logan pushed away from the table. "I'm going out to feed the animals and then I'll help you with the dishes." He kissed her on the cheek. "That roast was delicious. You should talk to Ma, though, she could tell you what she does to hers."

Elli looked at the door Logan just closed behind him and wanted to throw her plate at it, but she didn't. *I'd just have to clean it up.* She wanted to either throw the plate, or throw *herself* in Logan's arms and tell him she loved him—she just couldn't decide which she wanted to do most. He treated her well and made sure she had everything she needed, but she longed to hear those three words from him, but wasn't sure she ever would.

Sighing, she gathered the dishes and poured the hot water from the stove into the wash pan. She could be almost done by the time Logan came in, and they'd still have time to sit on the porch and watch the sun go down.

That was the most peaceful part of her day, especially now that she was expecting and so very tired from working hard all day long.

"Start getting ready, we've waited long enough and the town won't be expecting it now. I went close to town and didn't see a soul watching that bank."

"Alvin, I'm telling you I have a bad feeling about this town. Something isn't right." Dusty had the same feeling every time his brother mentioned Trace Hollow. This wasn't the small town Alvin should look to steal from.

"You're as bad as those boys. I say we're doing it. Now, find the boys and listen up. I have a plan."

Dusty sighed and went to gather the boys. *Life isn't meant to be like this for two young boys. Matter of fact, it isn't meant to be like this for me, either.*

His shoulders slumped as he went to find his nephews. He simply had to find a way out from under Alvin's thumb and take the boys with him. Alvin always did the robberies by himself, but the day was coming that he was going to want all of them to do more than be lookouts.

Even if he doesn't, what lessons am I teaching the boys by participating at all?

Dusty found the boys reading the books that had once belonged to their mother. They were sitting beside the creek just being boys with no responsibilities.

As they should be.

11

"Everyone is staring at me," Elli whispered as she walked into church on Logan's arm.

"Well, of course they are! You're the prettiest woman in the whole town."

Elli's cheeks heated at his words as they sat down. The little church was filling up fast.

"Won't be long until we've outgrown this little building. By the time all your sisters get here, we're going to have to add on," Uncle George said, patting her shoulder as he walked by.

"Seems to me, we're going to need a whole *new* church. In a few years, maybe a new school too. This town is growing, and with all these women coming...it's a real blessing!" Faye said after turning to Elli, who'd been led to the pew directly behind her.

Elli agreed with a smile and a nod, then sighed from a sudden feeling of exhaustion. She was relieved when church began and she could sit and relax as she listened. The music soothed her and she'd quickly found she loved hearing Pastor Don speak. He didn't deliver his sermons the same way his brother in Ohio did. Yet, they both got the good Lord's message across equally well. Pastor Don *never* raised his voice and was more of a storyteller. When he preached, he would read a verse and relate it to something personal from his life.

Elli found herself laughing as he told a story of how several boys at his old church in Winchester overturned an outhouse, with the pastor's wife inside.

"Now, what I'm leading to, is that sin is sin. Those boys grew up and were forgiven, and I would know. My brother and I were two of those boys. That's the gift God graces to all of us. All you need to do is ask for His forgiveness. No matter if your sin is turning over an outhouse or murder, it still falls under His ten commandments. I want you all to remember that this week. We will still face our punishments here on earth, but through His grace, we are forgiven. We don't need to earn it or deserve it. God graces us with forgiveness the moment we are sincere and ask for it."

The service passed much too quickly. Elli could have listened to more of Pastor Don's stories, and the weather was cooler, which made her feel better. It had rained overnight, just enough to take away the humidity and help the crops, but not enough to muddy the roads.

After the last hymn, Pastor Don announced they had some town business to discuss. The children were sent outside to play and the sound of whispered questions filled the room.

"Normally, we take business decisions to the town council," Pastor Don began. "However, this will be a bigger decision than usual. We—the town council, that is—have decided it's time to elect a mayor. Trace Hollow needs a leader. The mayor would be the decision-maker among us." The men of the council nodded in agreement, and he took a deep breath before asking the next question. "The town council discussed it. We decided to take nominations and vote today. Is there a nomination?"

More whispers wove throughout the room.

"I nominate George Hughes!" Logan called out as he stood.

Elli was proud of her husband and his Uncle George.

"Are there any other nominations?" Pastor Don looked nervous as he spoke, and Elli just couldn't imagine why.

"Oh, I don't think so, Pastor," came from the 'Amen corner' of the church. Thelma Hall was *not happy* about something, once again. She and her sister, Ethel, were never happy and, more often than not, argued just for the sake of arguing.

Elli listened, confused, as the church collectively sighed.

"That's right, sister. We need to have an election not a quick vote. This town is growing and we should elect a mayor just like the bigger cities do." Ethel Young nodded her head once, as if punctuating her statement, and crossed her arms. Thelma and Ethel were there when the town was founded. They were both widowed and spent most of their time meddling in other folks' business. Elli hadn't been to a town meeting before, but she'd heard enough about them. Every time a new idea was brought forward, Thelma and Ethel would find fault with it.

I wonder why two such kindhearted women are inclined to complain so much?

The two sisters would feed anyone, even strangers, and had appeared at Elli's door with gifts the day after they heard about the baby.

They also complained about everything from the weather to the president's wife—the weather was either *too* rainy, *too* hot, or *too* cold, depending on the time of year and the current president's wife was too young for their taste. Elli often felt like she should repent for her thoughts about the two, whenever alone with them for very long.

"I don't hear any other nominations. Is there anyone else who would like to run for mayor?" Pastor Don, one of the sweetest men alive in Elli's eyes, ran his finger under his collar as though agitated.

"Jack? Stan? *Anyone?*"

"Doesn't really seem to be a point in me running. I'd just vote for George anyway," Jack said while rubbing his chin in thought.

"I always thought George had the knowhow with numbers and got along well with people. It should be him running the town." Deacon Stan crossed his arms and matched stares with Ethel.

"I guess we just won't have a mayor until someone else decides to run so we can have an election," Thelma said and crossed her arms with a *hmph*.

"They're worse than children," Elli whispered to Logan.

"It's been this way for as long as I can remember. For two women, they sure can cause an uproar. If their husbands were alive, this wouldn't happen. Women should do what they're told and vote the way their husbands tell them to."

"*What* did you just say?" Elli asked, her voice pitched a little too loud.

Elli could see Logan's face pinch and she knew he was confused by her sudden change in personality.

"What didn't you hear? Women vote the way their husbands tell them. What's wrong with that? In most states, women can't vote at all."

"Women can vote any way they want to, *Sheriff*," Elli said with ice in her voice, plenty loud enough for everyone to hear.

"Well, of course they can," Emma said.

"Faye always votes the way I do," Deacon Stan said, a little too smugly.

"We have voted exactly *once* since women began voting here, and I just happened to agree with your opinion. We did need to build boardwalks in front of the buildings. It had nothing to do with what you '*told me to do,*'" Faye informed him, planting her hands on her hips.

With widening eyes, her husband began backing away.

"I guarantee Margie would vote my way," George stated, as if it were a well-known fact.

"You would do *best* to stop thinking then. I happen to agree you would be a fine mayor, but if we voted on something and I disagreed with you, I would vote my own way." Margie took a step to stand united with Elli, Emma, and Faye.

Frannie eyed Jack through narrowed eyes. "Do *you* have an opinion on this matter, dear?" she asked, ever so sweetly, and batting her eyelids at him for good measure.

Deacon Jack looked at the women and chose his words carefully before he spoke. He could picture the empty dinner tables and piles of dirty clothes all over town when the men were expected do it all themselves.

"Why, I believe anyone can vote however they want! That's what voting is all about."

The men erupted in argument and all the women stood together.

"I'll run for mayor."

The church was silent for a moment as they all looked around to find the man the voice had come from.

"Over here!"

"Zeb? What are you doing in that window?" Logan asked after spotting the man first.

"Listening to the preacher. I like the music, too."

"Why didn't you just come in like everyone else?"

"I can hear just fine sitting here on my crate, and I don't have to get involved in all the gossip and arguing that goes on."

"Well, why are you standing in the window *now*?" George threw his hands in the air, his face turning slightly red.

"He's *there*, because he just declared himself a candidate for mayor. *You* heard him, didn't you, *Sheriff*?" Elli held Logan's gaze.

"I heard him, all right. You sure you want to do this, Zeb? Can you even stay sober long enough to run a campaign?"

"He won't have to run his own campaign," Elli announced and stepped toward the window. "We'll run it for him."

The women moved to stand by Elli and Zeb, who stood looking in from outside the church. Thelma and Ethel both wore satisfied smiles.

The men still stood in the aisle of the church, scratching their heads, and wondering exactly how all this got started.

Pastor Don remained by the pulpit holding Helen's hand, his eyes closed, praying this disruption wouldn't leave a lasting harmful effect on the marriages in their town—especially the newest one.

12

It was only Tuesday and Logan missed his wife. Last Sunday, after the meeting about a new mayor, they'd eaten lunch in silence. He'd even had to make himself a sandwich from the leftover meat for supper. Monday morning, she hadn't made his breakfast *or* his lunch, and he'd had to eat at the boardinghouse— where Margie even charged him for his meal for the first time! She'd charged every man for their meal, including George!

"I'll be in town today with your ma," Elli said flatly.

"I thought your ladies' meetings were on Thursdays?"

"It's not a ladies' meeting, it's a campaign meeting."

Logan finished his milk and stared sadly down at the breakfast he'd scrounged up for himself, *again*, this morning—cold hard biscuits, a jar of jam, and the milk he'd brought in from the barn.

"Elli, I don't want things to be like this. We all know Uncle George is the best choice for mayor.

Zeb can't take care of *himself*, much less the whole town."

Elli turned toward the dishpan and washed her own dishes that had held her meal of bacon, eggs, and a warm fresh biscuit...with a nice heaping of homemade gravy piled on it. She'd made herself the biscuit just that morning. That's right. Only *one* biscuit. All the women had agreed to stop cooking and cleaning for the men until the men realized just how much the women actually did. Women had to make choices every single day, by weighing what was best for their families and their community. Why shouldn't they have a say in the matter of who runs the town, and their opinions be considered just as important as the men's?

Well, everyone *except* Frannie and Deacon Jack. He was the only man smart enough to agree with his wife. Although Elli was sure he only did it to save himself from the arguments he saw going on all around him.

"I don't want things to be like this either, Logan. I'm also not going to live my life doing everything you say, whether I agree or not."

"Elli, the Bible says you're supposed to follow your husband," Logan declared, then took a deep breath, his chest puffing out with a self-importance that made Elli want to fling the pan at his head.

"Why, *Sheriff*, you're absolutely right."

This wasn't good. Her tone was too sweet, and she had a strange look on her beautiful face. She also knew he hated when she called him 'Sheriff.'

"So, you just leave a list of orders for me to do today, and I'll be sure they're done—one way or another."

Without another word, Logan stood, placed his empty cup in the wash pan, then grabbed his hat and left.

Elli watched out the window as he came out of the barn, already riding Sampson, and turned toward town.

I love him. She curved her arms around her slight baby bump, then sat at the table and cried. Elli had known she wouldn't be able to keep up the charade of being a good Christian wife and keep her temper in check forever, but she'd hoped she could do it long enough for Logan to love her first.

Laying her head on the table, she let her tears flow until there were none left. Elli finally stood and washed her face of tears, then straightened herself to go to town for the first of Zeb's campaign meetings.

She'd taken her stand, and now she had to stick with it...whether she liked the results or not.

———

"I think Elli should be in charge since she was the one who initially stood up for women's right to vote independently from their husbands!" a voice called out from the back of the room.

Elli looked, but couldn't be sure who'd said it. They'd decided to use the town meeting room beside the general store—with Uncle George's blessing— and it was a good thing they did, because there wasn't a single woman from Trace Hollow not in

119

attendance. Word had spread quickly, and even the prairie women had shown up.

"I agree," Emma said. "All in favor?"

To Elli's amazement, every woman in the room called, "Aye!"

With every eye on her, she cleared her throat. "I think we should start making some signs. We could use the ropes they hung the Independence Day signs with to hang these from." Having been the oldest, Elli was used to bossing children around at the orphanage, so taking charge didn't bother her at all, but overseeing a group of full-grown women *was* something new, and maybe a bit intimidating.

"That's a wonderful idea. Eunice and Beth made those signs, and I'm sure they can make these too." Emma's voice held pride as she looked at her daughter-in-law.

"Thought we were gonna have cookies or something at this shindig?"

Elli rolled her eyes. The guest of honor had finally arrived.

Zeb strolled in the door like he owned the place. Unshaven, unwashed, and smelling like corn liquor.

That was exactly what the women expected, and they were prepared for it.

"Well, there you are, Zeb! We've been waiting for you." Elli hoped her face looked welcoming.

"Had to come. Faye said she would come find me, else."

"What I *said* was, I had better *not* have to come looking for the likes of you. You volunteered to run, we didn't ask you to." Faye moved slowly toward Frannie as she spoke.

"What do I need to do? I need to sign sumthin'?"

"You certainly do. Ethan, our town lawyer, drew up an official paper for all candidates to sign and then we have a few other things you need to do." Elli pulled a chair out for him, and the women circled around him.

"All I can do is an 'X' for my name."

"That's good enough for us," Elli told him as he sat down. She moved the cookies just out of his reach. "Sign first."

Zeb eyed the cookies and the steam coming off the cup of coffee sitting beside them. He drew an X on the paper where Elli pointed and she slid the plate toward him.

He ate the cookies and drank the coffee between bites, making sure there wasn't a crumb left, then attempted to stand. "I guess we're done here."

"I don't think so, Zeb. We have just a few more things to do."

Zeb finally realized he'd been trapped by the women. Circled and outnumbered, his eyes widened as he took in the items spread about the room. He sobered up quite quickly, and it *wasn't* because of the coffee.

A washtub stood in the corner of the room with steam rolling out of it. Beside it, was a small table and chair, and Zeb was *sure* he saw a razor and brush.

Panic set in.

"Now hold it right there, ladies! I agreed to run for mayor, I *didn't* agree to losing my beard! I been growing it for years."

"We can't be having our candidate looking like...well, looking like a moonshiner." Elli motioned the other women to move in closer.

"Now wait just *one* minute—"

Elli stood as straight and tall as she could, and in her firmest tone said, "We will not wait another single minute. A little soap and water never hurt a soul, and you, *sir*, are getting in that tub...*one way or another.*"

Zeb only hesitated for a moment. "All right, Elli, since it's you asking."

She couldn't believe it worked! He walked right over to the chair where Emma waited to shave him and sat down. The other ladies moved the partition so he could bathe in privacy. New clothes were stacked beside the tub.

"Now, just a little off, Emma. It took me a long time to grow these whiskers."

"It all goes, Zeb." Elli stood firm.

Zeb blinked a couple of times, swallowed, then nodded miserably.

Pleasure filled Elli as her mother-in-law took off every whisker on his face. She'd made her point with Zeb, and she'd done it without losing her temper.

What she *hadn't* seen were Faye and Frannie standing behind her, but Zeb could see them quite clearly. The women held very scary-looking, sharp bristled scrub brushes and lye soap, and were more than willing to use them...and Zeb knew it.

Zeb walked out from behind the partition, and a collective gasp came from those in the room, but little Kaitlyn Martin summed it up best.

"Good heavens! Zeb's hair *ain't* brown, it's blond like mine! He don't stink no more, either."

"*Isn't* brown and he *doesn't* stink *anymore*," her mother corrected the young girl.

"See? Ma thinks so too, Mr. Zeb. I'm proud of you!"

"Oh, Zeb, you look wonderful!" Elli approved. He now looked like a respectable candidate should.
Wearing a new black suit with tie, a crisp white shirt and new boots, Zeb looked like a different man.

"Only took four tubs of water," Faye remarked dryly, but the satisfied expression on her face indicated she thought it was worth it.

Margie held up the mirror she'd brought with her, and Zeb took a good look at himself, a small tear forming in his eye. "You ladies did a real fine job of cleaning me up. I guess I'll be on my way while you finish your meeting."

"Not quite yet, Zeb. We have a few more things to go over with you. If we intend to have a real campaign, you have some work to do yourself." Elli crossed her arms as the other women positioned themselves to block any escape he might try to make.

"Now, Elli, I offered to run for mayor, I didn't say I was going to turn into a saint!"

"Zeb, I don't expect you to be a saint." Elli narrowed her eyes. "What I *do* expect, is for you to make yourself, and all these women, proud that you're a candidate, and I have *just* the plan to do that."

Zeb's whiskers were gone and every emotion that passed over his face was easy to read now. He knew what she was talking about.

The town moonshiner was going dry until the election was over.

*****

After the ladies laid down the law to Zeb, they held a quick march through town to show him off. The men stared. They weren't sure who he was.

Herbie had somehow gotten loose again, and followed them with what might have been a suspicious look, if geese could look suspicious.

Logan had a clear view from his office window when they walked out of the meeting room. He was about to walk over to the mercantile to talk to George, when he saw his uncle already heading toward his own office. They met at the door and watched as the women marched by for the second time.

"Zeb is all cleaned up, Sheriff." Kaitlyn identified the man to everyone she passed with a regal tone.

For a seven-year-old, she has an awfully big attitude.

"Even Herbie isn't interested in you today." George snickered as he saw the goose trailing behind the women.

"I guess we can find at least one blessing in just about everything."

"You think there are enough women voters that Zeb could actually win, Logan?"

Logan twisted his beard. "I'm only sure of two things, Uncle George. We'd better make sure every man available votes. We have fewer women, but they're *all* going to show up."

"What's the second?"

Logan shook his head sadly as he watched his wife leading the procession. "It takes a while to be a good husband and know when to keep your mouth shut."

"You're learning, Logan. You're learning."

13

Logan called a meeting with the men at the church the next afternoon, and the women assumed it was about the election. It wasn't.

"It doesn't make sense to me that Spy Run's bank was robbed like this. First, there were only scratches by the lock, which is a rather poor attempt to get in. Then, a full clean-out of the bank while it was under watch. Now, three more towns nearby have been hit. At Dry Hollow's bank, the watchman was shot. He lived and was able to give a description of the man who shot him and his shooter's accomplice. I'm passing around the wanted poster. It was the infamous Jones brothers, gentlemen. They're both tall with black hair and matching beards. They apparently prefer to dress in all black as well. We need to start setting up shifts in order to keep full-time watch on our bank."

"I can take a shift, Sheriff, but I don't know that we can hide this from our wives." Doc Matt looked concerned.

"I don't think we *should* hide it from them, but I figured a meeting with the entire town attending might draw attention if anyone is watching. This meeting could easily have been about the election. Each of us should go home and explain it to the women."

"Well, at least the ones who have a woman still speaking to him." George looked sadly around the room.

"Easy way to fix Margie not talking to you, George, is to give her a ring. Then you'll wish she'd stop talking!" Jack told him, then snorted with laughter.

"Sure, you laugh, even though you kept quiet when we all knew you agreed with us at the meeting for mayor," Stan pointed out to Jack in disgust. Stan was not a happy man. In fact, any time Faye wasn't happy, Stan's misery was guaranteed.

"Look, none of us are happy right now," Logan stated wearily, running his hand through his blond curls. He needed them cut again, but didn't want to ask Elli or his ma.

"You started the whole thing, Sheriff," Stan shot back.

Several voices muttered agreement.

"He didn't do anything that any one of you wouldn't have, he simply said it first. Sheriff just happened to be in a meeting where all the women could side together, and we were all dumb enough to get involved."

Logan shot Uncle George a grateful look for standing up for him.

More murmurs of agreement came grudgingly through the room.

"Let's consider this settled. The list to sign up for watch is on the table. Mark your name and remember your time."

"Somebody sign me up and tell me when." A voice said from the window.

"Zeb, why can't you just walk into the church and do it yourself?" Logan was growing tired of Zeb. He was sober and not sitting in a cell, which was a good thing, but he was smack dab in the middle of Logan's biggest problem.

"If you want me in the room, don't have these meetings in the church. I might be dressed for it, but it would take an act of God to get me through that door."

"That's exactly what I'm praying for, Zeb. An act of God." Pastor Don folded his hands together as if he meant to start praying exactly that, right then.

"Should I be afraid? Should I worry about them breaking into the house too?"

Logan knew the same questions asked by his wife were being asked by many women all over town. He'd stopped and talked to the Trace sisters, but Bobbie and Jan weren't afraid. They had their animals to alert them to any strangers and both had been raised in the west. They may appear sweet and innocent, but both women could shoot and take care of themselves just fine.

The deacons had agreed to stop at a few other homes without husbands to warn them. Eunice was a widow who sold baked goods in town, and said she'd keep her eyes open for anything, or anyone, unusual.

Logan's thoughts turned back to his young wife and her questions. "All I'm asking is that you keep your guard up. I'll be taking extra shifts, and I'd like Ma to come in and stay here on the nights I'm out."

Elli considered it as she refilled their coffee cups once more. "I can agree to that. I wish Sophia was here already."

"Now why would you wish that? She would only want to be with her own husband."

"You don't have to snap at me."

"Elli, I can't say anything right to you anymore. Maybe I should just stop talking to you."

"Maybe you *should*. I'm certainly tired of the things you have to say." Elli turned away to stare out the window.

"I'll just go on out to Ma's and make sure she's been informed and ask if she'll come in."

"You do that, *Sheriff*." Elli snapped. "While you're at it, make sure she cooks your dinner before you leave, since you always tell me to talk to her about my cooking."

Logan grabbed his hat on his way out and slammed the door behind him.

Logan made a stop before leaving town. He asked Sam and Lucy, his nearest neighbors, to keep an eye on his house. He was worried about Elli and the baby.

"I'll go on over and visit with her, Sheriff." Lucy wiped her hands on her apron.

"I'd appreciate that, Lucy," Logan told her, then left the house and returned to his horse. Since Sampson always listened to his problems without judging, Logan took advantage of his poor horse all the way to his ma's.

"I understand what's going on in town. Now tell me what's *really* wrong, son."

"Nothing else, Ma. Just making sure you and the hands know we need to be on guard. I'm going out to have Brandon loan me some men." He walked toward the front door.

"Logan James, stop right there."

She didn't raise her voice, nor did she have a wooden spoon, but he obeyed immediately at her use of his full name.

"Look me in the eye and tell me nothing more is wrong. Sampson didn't even want to be around you, if him running off to the barn the moment you got your hind-end off his back is anything to go by, and that horse normally loves you like Herbie does."

"I can't tell you, Ma."

"There is nothing you can tell me that would make me love you less. I loved you before you were born, just like you love your child and my soon-to-be grandchild."

"Elli hates me."

"Elli does *not* hate you. She loves you, Logan."

"She told me to leave and said to have you cook my dinner since I'm always telling her to talk to you. I can't believe she would even bring that up, Ma! I try to show I care about her and that I want to help, at *every* meal, by telling her she should talk to you about her cooking and—."

"Wait." Emma held up her hand. "What *exactly* do you say at every meal?"

"I say the food was good and she should talk to you about your recipes." Fire lit up Emma's eyes.

"Now, Ma, you *know* my Elli is a fine cook. It's those spices she uses, that you don't, which makes it so good and I thought you'd like—"

"Logan, we've determined Elli is a *great* cook. I'm happy to admit she out-cooks me every day." Emma sighed. "The *problem* is how you're saying it. I believe Elli must think you want *me* to teach *her* to cook." She sighed and swept some crumbs from her table.

"Stop shaking your head at me, Ma. There's no reason she would think that, because I'm quite clear what I mean. She's choosing to misunderstand just to pick fights with me."

"Logan, I love you, son...but you have a habit of saying things that only make sense to one person and that is yourself. Elli is a wonderful wife. She takes very good care of you. Go talk to her, and from now on, stop talking after you tell her how good the meal was. Don't include a thing about me. That's one misunderstanding I'll clear up with Elli on your behalf. I'll go and talk to her about it, but *you* will fix the rest. Give her a chance, son.
She loves you."

"She doesn't love me. She's never said it."

"Have *you* said it to her?"

Lightning went off in Logan's head. *Have I told her I love her?* He *did* love his wife, and he assumed she knew it.

"I have to go, Ma. Send Brandon over, would you?" He kissed her cheek and yelled his thanks as he ran out the door.

Emma watched as he hastily grabbed the horse's reins and mounted him. Sampson appeared to feel the urgency and that his master was back to normal, as he took off for town.

I've raised a good son, Lord. Help him do this right.

She went out to the barn to get Brandon and decided she might as well go to town now and make sure her son managed to get himself out of this mess...and not make it worse.

"We're going to hit the bank after dark." Alvin Clayton was already counting the money he planned to steal.

"When the bank in Spy Run was robbed, it was only dusk. We'll wait until the middle of the night to break in. We're going to town early and we're going to eat supper and make sure the whole town is comfortable. I'm not worried about showing our faces. I'm not wanted anywhere, since no one ever looks for a pickpocket. The sheriff will blame the Jones Gang. They'll never suspect us."

"You know, we *could* get jobs..." Dusty said, looking at his hands as he spoke.

"Doing what? I can barely read, and my back won't hold up to working a ranch or farm."

"It might if you stopped drinking, Uncle Alvin," Dylan spoke up without thinking.

"Watch your smart mouth, boy! I'm the reason you eat around here."

"Alvin, they're going to be watching the bank." Dusty wanted him to think about the risk and get his attention off their nephew.

"One sheriff? He'll be home sleeping. He has that pretty, young wife to take care of."

"Uncle Alvin, the folks are nice there. I don't want to steal from them," Codyn said bravely, both his and Dylan's eyes gleamed with tears.

"That's enough of the caterwauling. You two don't do the stealing anyway, so it's none of your concern. You're only there to make sure I don't get caught. If we get enough tonight, we never have to steal again."

None of them believed him, but they all headed to the cold creek to wash up. They were going to town.

14

Logan made good time between his ma's ranch and back to his own home. He opened the door to his house and called out, but the house was empty, and without Elli in it, it felt cold.

He shut the door again and headed into town.

Lucy treated Elli to dinner at the boardinghouse. Margie had already fed the miners, so the tables were empty, until Codyn and Dylan walk in with two men. Elli was thrilled to see the boys.

Codyn introduced his uncles to Elli, and she introduced Lucy to them.

"You look familiar to me," Dusty told Lucy.

"People say that to me all the time. Must be someone out there that looks like me."

She then ducked quickly into the kitchen with Margie.

"You all eat your fill. I'm going to pay for your dinner this evening." Elli smiled at them in invitation, glad she could help the boys find nourishment.

"Ma'am, we can't let you do that," Dusty said, his face turning red with embarrassment.

"Now, Dusty," Alvin interrupted him. "Are you trying to take away this nice lady's blessing? The Good Book says it's blessed to give."

Elli beamed. "It certainly does, and anyone who has been raising such fine boys as these deserves a dinner out."

After she'd eaten, Elli offered to help Margie with the dishes.

"I won't hear of it. Faye and Stan, Jack and Frannie, they're all out walking. You and Lucy should take a walk before it gets much darker. It's going to be cold sooner than you think, so go out and enjoy the air."

Lucy agreed, so the two women decided to walk to the church and watch the sunset over the mountains.

Logan got to town and looked for Lucy's wagon.

There's no way Lucy took her to the saloon. Elli still hasn't gotten comfortable with the idea of even walking in there for the music.

He tied Sampson up and decided to walk. He had a plan. He'd find his wife and announce to her and the whole town he loved her, but he only made it to the corner past his office when he spotted a dark figure with a gun creeping around the corner of the bank.

Lord, help me. It looks like most of the town is out tonight.

Logan managed to wave and get Uncle George's attention when he stepped out onto the porch of the general store.

"How many men you think we have in town and can get here without us having to ring the church bell?"

George shook his head, frowning. "Most of them are scattered about town. The store has been busy for the past hour with folks talking, walking, and visiting. They know the weather could turn anytime, so they're taking advantage this evening. The men are still trying to make up with their wives."

"Gather as many as you can, as quietly as you can, and get the women off the street—"

A female voice cried out, from the direction of the bank, cutting Logan's sentence off.

Logan ran toward the bank, along with other townsfolk. There they discovered a man in black outside, with a gun in his right hand, and the pastor's wife standing in front of him.

"You need to repent right now, son. Drop that silly gun and I'll pray with you. The good Lord will forgive anything, you know. In fact, just last Sunday my hus—"

The criminal grabbed the older woman and turned her, his left arm holding Helen tight against him as he stared at Logan and the small crowd that was gathering.

"Well, for heaven's sake! At least let me hand someone my blackberry cobbler. It took me hours to make this. I was doing the Lord's work and taking it to someone who's bedridden."

"Lady, hold still," the man ordered gruffly. "You wouldn't be the first person I've shot with this gun."

Logan drew his gun and aimed it steadily at the criminal. The problem was Helen kept moving and waving her skillet full of cobbler.

He couldn't risk hitting her, and the man was backed into a corner between the bank and the blacksmith. There was no way out for him and he knew it, which was why he'd taken a hostage.

"If you shoot me, I'll go to heaven. Oh, what a glorious day that will be when I go!" Helen started singing hymns loud and off-key.

"Drop the cobbler and shut up, lady!"

"You want me to waste food? That would be a sin. Faye, I see you out there. Come get my cobbler and give it to the Martins if I die. Old lady Kaitlyn isn't feeling well. You know she used to be able to raise without ropes? Not to mention the fireworks that woman caused everywhere she went!"

Logan thought Helen had finally lost her mind. *Old lady Kaitlyn? Raise without ropes? What in the world is wrong with her head? Must be the shock.*

"Absolutely, Helen." Faye said, from behind Logan.

Logan snarled in response, "You certainly are *not.*"

"You heard her, Sheriff. She wants me to take the cobbler."

"Faye, we have one woman in danger, we don't need two."

"Save your words, Logan. I am going to get that pie."

Logan attempted to grab the deacon's wife as she passed him, but couldn't take his aim off of the man who held the preacher's wife.

"Don't mind me, I'm just collecting the cobbler," she announced as she walked right up to them.

"What is *wrong* with the women in this town?" the man in black asked the sheriff in disbelief.

"Hand over the cobbler, Helen. He can't shoot both of us," Faye said directly to her friend, a smile tight across her face.

"Faye, you're such a dear. Just make sure Kaitlyn gets this. She'll be well enough soon to be roping again."

"Oh, I'm sure she'll be doing it soon."

Logan saw Brandon creeping toward him from the back of the blacksmith. Brandon pointed up, and Logan figured he was pointing at the second floor of the building across the street. George would have positioned himself or someone else there.

He figured wrong.

From the top of the bank, several objects flew into view. It was the Brown and Martin boys, and they came swinging in on ropes above the man and his captive.

Helen dropped to the ground when the explosions began.

Fireworks?

Somewhere, the boys had found leftover fireworks. Helen's captor thought they were firing guns at him. He dropped beside Helen and covered his head, his gun clattering across the boardwalk well out of his reach. After they'd dropped the fireworks and landed on the ground, the boys scattered but Logan saw them peeking around the corner of one of the buildings.

"Get him up," Logan ordered Brandon. Brandon did and restrained him with the help of a few other men.

"*Logan!*" His name was called from a voice filled with fear and his heart clenched.

He turned to see another man, a duplicate to the one on the ground, but this one held Elli in front of him.

Logan didn't think he'd ever known such terror.

"Let her go," he ordered.

The man laughed deeply and said, "I don't think so, Sheriff. You're going to let my brother go, and we'll walk out of here with this woman. Don't worry, we'll leave her outside town and she can find her way back once we're gone. No posse. We're walking away safe and sound."

"The Jones Brothers," Lucy proclaimed with a tinge of awe and fear in her voice. Everyone knew who they were. Tales of the Jones Brothers' train robberies filled the newspapers the general store received.

The entire crowd fell silent until Codyn asked innocently, "Uncle Alvin, I thought *you* were going to rob the bank?"

"We have two sets of criminals in town?" Faye asked, her voice rising with each word.

The man holding Elli turned to see who Codyn was talking to.

It only took that one second of distraction, and the now-standing Helen grabbed her skillet out of Faye's hand, swung, and hit Elli's captor on the side of his head.

He dropped both Elli and his gun, and began cussing while wiping cobbler from his face.

In the commotion, the first man fought free and kicked Brandon's hand, causing him to drop his own gun. The outlaw threw himself to the ground, grabbed the gun, and before Brandon could stop him, fired one shot toward Logan.

Logan was able to fire a clear shot too.

Both shots connected.

15

Brandon had the second of the Jones brothers locked up tight inside the jail. The man was still covered in sticky blackberry cobbler, and Brandon threatened to shoot him if he didn't stop whining about it.

The two shooting victims were rushed to Doc Matt's office, where Matt's wife Angela, and a few of the other woman helped him deliver medical aid to both.

The entire town crowded in and around the outside of Doc's office to await news. Word had spread quickly, and even the folks that hadn't witnessed the shootings were there for support.

Elli and Emma sobbed, while Bobbie and Jan Trace comforted them. After all, God couldn't be done with him yet.

Angela came out from the small room, her face flushed, blood splattered on her shoes, and announced, "We lost the Jones brother. Logan's bullet hit exactly where he aimed. I promise to be back with more news soon." She took Elli's and squeezed it. "Keep praying, sweetheart. I promise we're doing all we can for him."

Later, when she came out to see Elli and Emma again, a small smile curved her lips. The second surgery had gone well, but now the real waiting would begin.

The next morning, Lucy finally insisted Elli eat and wash her face. "I won't hear any excuses. We're going to the saloon to get some food in you since Margie's here with George. It's closer than your own home, and you'll feel better. Emma will send for us if you're needed."

Emma nodded at Elli to go on. "For your child and my grandchild, please eat. Logan would want you to take care of both of you."

Elli agreed with a reluctant nod, then she and Lucy left Emma in the office to wait with all their friends. As the two women walked slowly toward the saloon, Elli felt more of the regret that had been plaguing her since last night. She had only seen Logan briefly, and

she was ashamed of the way she'd been behaving with the election, and even her attitude toward his preference for his mother's cooking over hers.

"I don't deserve my husband, my friends here, *or* this town, Lucy. I've been behaving horribly at home."

Lucy laughed for the first time since the shooting. "Elli, I don't worry anymore about what I deserve. God's blessed me with a good husband, a wonderful town to live in, and many friends. *That* is what I focus on, and what you should be focusing on too. Most people don't feel they deserve the blessings they have."

"Lucy, can I ask why you don't go to church with us?"

"Sam and I tried to go when we first arrived. A few folks weren't too happy about saloon owners sitting in the same pew as them, or even in the same church. We talked to Pastor Don and Helen, and they understood. We have a Bible study on Sunday morning instead, so we still worship."

"You can sit with me any time you'd like to try to attend church again."

"Thank you, Elli, but I'd rather stay home than make folks uncomfortable. They may decide to stop going, and in my way of thinking, they're the ones who need God most."

They entered the saloon and Elli looked around. Logan was right. The inside was clean and nothing at all like the seedy places she'd heard about. Sam stood behind the bar and their only customer was Zeb. He held a mug in his hand and Elli felt disappointment when she saw it.

"Root beer, Elli. Told ya I would stay sober for you and the other women, and I'm doing it." Zeb raised his glass in her direction.

"Truth." Sam said. "He's been here all night, waiting to hear something and drinking root beer."

I did it again! I thought the worst about someone without knowing the facts first.

"I'm sorry I doubted you, Zeb."

"Oh, I'll fail you again, Elli. I just won't do it until the election is over."

She laughed a little at that. Zeb truly had a kind heart and at least he was honest.

"Follow me, Elli." Lucy took her through the kitchen and into their living quarters, which also was very clean and orderly. She brought Elli a pan of water and a cloth to wash up with.

"I'm going to go check on Sam and the sandwiches. He's making enough to take back

Elli

to the doc's office so we can feed everyone, including Zeb."

Elli wanted to tell her thank you, but her eyes filled with tears instead.

"That's enough of that. He's going to be fine. You and Logan will work things out and that baby of yours will be perfect."

"I sure hope so, Lucy. I sure hope so."

<hr />

Elli walked back to the doc's office with Zeb, who carried a large basket of fried egg and sausage sandwiches. They were still several steps from Doc's when the door flew open and Emma ran out yelling, "He's awake!"

Elli gasped, then ran right inside. She approached the bed slowly to catch her breath, then dropped in the chair next to him and stroked her finger lovingly down his cheek.

"Thank you, Herbie. You saved my husband's life."

The goose croaked a small, weak quack in response. At the last moment, Herbie had jumped into the line of fire. In a flurry of feathers, the brave goose took the bullet meant for Logan. Logan had rushed the other Jones brother to jail while Elli followed the others to Doc Matt's to wait for news on Herbie.

"I think he's going to make it. He'll need a quiet place for recovery, though. The Trace sisters don't have the time to give him the care he's going to need with all their other animals to take care of as well," Doc told her, his expression showing both exhaustion and relief that his unique patient had made it through surgery.

"He can stay at our house. I'll get a pen built beside the back steps."

At Logan's voice, Elli's heart leaped with joy. Without a second thought, she stood and turned, then ran into his arms.

"Logan, I'm so sorry!"

"*You're* sorry? I'm the one that's sorry. I've been a fool, Elli. I love you."

Elli froze at those three words. Logan had changed her life by sending for and marrying her, but now she had everything she had ever hoped for.

"I love you, Logan. We have a lot to talk about."

"We sure do...right after I tell Herbie thank you."

Elli was positive the goose winked at her as Logan told him he was now going to be living with them.

16

Two days later, election day had arrived for Trace Hollow. The voting was set up in the meeting room beside the general store, and folks wandered in all day to cast their votes. Ethan, the town's attorney, would count them once it was closed and announce the winner.

George kept away from the room and stayed in the general store, as he didn't want to be accused of trying to gain votes, and Zeb sat inside the store with him, playing checkers with anyone who was interested in a game.

"Zeb, if you won today, what would be the first thing you would do as mayor?" Stan asked.

"He'd make moonshine legal," Jack answered, laughing at his own joke.

"I would not." Zeb lifted his jaw, the pose defiant.

"Well, why not? That's how you make your living, isn't it?" Stan asked, drawing his eyebrows together.

"Cause if it was legal, I'd make *less* money and I'd have to pay taxes."

"Ya know, you're a smart businessman. If you put that to good use, you could be somebody, Zeb." Jack stated, as if the suit and haircut could make Zeb a changed man from the inside out.

"I already *am* somebody. The women think so, at least. I'll be suiting up for church from now on. Logan had some men build me a covered sitting station, right by my church window, after they built Herbie's new pen. I can sit there rain or shine, at least until the weather gets too cold."

"Wouldn't it be easier just to go inside the church?" George asked.

"Probably would, but I just don't want to. I rarely miss a Sunday, and I'm sure not missing any of Elli's sisters' weddings."

"Speaking of weddings...I have a favor to ask of you men." The twinkle was back in George's eye as he let them all in on a little secret he had planned.

Logan was on his way across the street to put in his vote, but got sidetracked by something he hoped to never see again.

"I don't care if you didn't actually rob the bank. You were still thinking about it," Helen yelled at Alvin while Faye sat on the poor man.

"What are you two *doing?*"

"Sharing the good news of Jesus, of course!" Faye didn't move an inch.

"He tried to get away, Sheriff, but Faye stopped him." Helen was indignant at the thought of someone trying to get away from them.

"Sheriff, I was only trying to leave town, and they *attacked* me!" The man's voice clearly expressed his outrage...but most prevalent, was his outright terror of the two fired-up women.

Logan could barely contain his laughter.

"We've been chasing him for two days, Sheriff. He's been a coward and wouldn't come out and face us." Faye looked as though she'd grown bored with the man now that the chase was over. She even smothered a yawn with one of her gloved hands!

"You're going to have to let him go, ladies. He *is* leaving town. Dusty and the boys are staying at the boardinghouse until they find a home of their own. Alvin here signed the papers Ethan drew up, letting Dusty adopt the boys."

"So there is some good in you then. You gave the boys to Dusty, as they should have been in the first place. Let him up, Faye."

Faye took her time, but she moved off him. She dusted herself off and turned to help the man up.

"No, thank you! I just want to get out of this town with all these crazy women and kids. What was going on with those boys flying through the air and dropping fireworks, anyway?" Alvin shook his head and spat on the ground as he brushed himself off.

"That wasn't the *boys'* idea. It was Kaitlyn Martin's. Emma and I heard her trying to talk her brothers and her neighbor's sons into setting them off earlier that week. When we realized we needed a distraction, I just started yelling and she knew what I wanted," Helen explained.

"You weren't worried about the boys getting hit by a stray bullet?" Alvin was incredulous at the thought process the women in this town had.

"We didn't know there was a twin to the first robber, and another pair of robbers, which was you and your own brother. The one holding me hadn't hurt me, so I didn't think he would really shoot anyone. I'll know better next time."

"*Next* time? I have to go, Sheriff. I have to get out of here!"

"You can go, Alvin. You aren't wanted anywhere that I know of. You'd best stay out of trouble, though. I sent out a telegram to be passed around with your description. Every lawman in these parts will know your name and what you look like, so the first pocket you pick, you'll be the first one they hunt down."

"This town... I'm never coming back to Trace Hollow."

"If you do, we'll see you at church. Just let us know and we'll save you a seat." Helen smiled so graciously that even Logan was amazed.

Alvin never looked back as he ran toward his horse.

That evening, Elli stood beside Logan and waited for Ethan to come out and announce the votes.

"This has certainly been an interesting election, Elli."

"It has. I do appreciate the time your ma took today to write down the dishes you liked, and then allowing me to help her by adding my own seasonings to the recipe."

"I should have been clearer when I talked to you about that."

"I should have spoken up instead of assuming."

Ethan came out then to stand on the steps of the mercantile for his announcement, and the entire town went silent.

"Would both our candidates come up here to stand with me? I think this was a hard-run campaign for Trace Hollow. We all learned many things, and it brought our community closer together...eventually."

George and Zeb shook hands, then hugged. It was a clean, fair race, and they both knew it.

"The winner, and new mayor of Trace Hollow, with one hundred percent of the votes is...George Hughes!"

Silence. It took a moment for the number to sink in.

"Zeb, did you forget to vote?" George asked.

"Of course not. I voted this morning."

"You didn't vote for yourself?"

"Now why would I do *that*? You're supposed to vote for the best man for the job. You're that man, George. I only ran for mayor to stop the arguing at church. I can't stand it when someone sticks their nose in just to cause trouble." He looked pointedly at Thelma and Ethel when he delivered that last bit.

"You don't think he means *us*, do you, Ethel?"

"Absolutely not. Everyone knows we only wanted a real election, and we got one. Now didn't we, sister?"

"There are better ways to get what you want," Bobbie Trace informed them.

"I'm awfully glad not *all* the sisters in town act like you two." Jan Trace crossed her arms and stared hard at Ethel and Thelma. "You created a fight among almost every couple in town, we had an election we didn't need...am I missing anything?"

"It all turned out well, and I think it's been good for the children to learn about voting and elections," Ethel stated.

Thelma sniffed in agreement with Ethel and they began to walk away, arms looped together to show a united front, when George called out for everyone to stay.

"As Mayor of Trace Hollow, I believe I'm missing one thing..." George's voice creaked slightly as he spoke.

"What's that, Mayor?" Ethan asked.

"A wife. Margie, will you marry me?"

"Land's sake! Of course, she will. You've kept us all waiting a long time for this." Faye elbowed Frannie to hush her. She didn't want to miss a word of this.

Dark-haired Margie walked up the few steps and quietly told him, "Yes."

"Will you marry me right away? *Now*? The church is ready, and so is Pastor Don."

Margie paled just slightly. She ran the boardinghouse and her clothes bore the stains of her workload. She hadn't even changed her apron from the busy day because she didn't want to miss the announcement when George became mayor, because she knew he would win. He was the best man for the job, and the townsfolk weren't fools.

The ladies understood her hesitation.

"Let me help with that," Emma said. "Give us an hour, George. She'll be ready."

Dusty, Codyn, and Dylan carried water to fill the tub while Emma and Elli showed Margie the dress they'd been sewing for her for weeks. They'd finished it just days ago.

"We knew it was going to happen, we just didn't know when." Elli was so happy to attend Logan's uncle's wedding. He and Margie were truly a match made in heaven.

The dress was light blue, and although it wasn't a fancy wedding dress, it was exactly what Margie had described the day of Elli's wedding—one she'd seen and loved in a catalog at the mercantile.

"It's perfect. Thank you!" Margie exclaimed, then fell silent.

Elli knew what it was like to simply not have words to describe the feelings of gratitude Margie felt. It happened to her daily.

Once Margie was ready, the group headed to the church.

———————

After Pastor Don announced the bride and groom as husband and wife, everyone shook hands with George and hugged Margie. They would have a potluck on Sunday after church to celebrate.

Dusty had served as a ranch cook before he'd left to care for his nephews, and now offered to take over the cooking at the boardinghouse, while Jack and Stan agreed to run the mercantile so the newlyweds could enjoy a couple days to themselves.

As they rode home after the wedding, Logan finally had a chance to ask Elli about the election.

"Elli, if you were going to vote for Uncle George anyway, why did you campaign for Zeb?"

"At first, it was because I was angry and stubborn. I firmly believe a woman can be a wife and support her husband, but still have a mind of her own. Later, it was because I saw something in Zeb. He might not stay cleaned up, and he'll probably still make moonshine, but deep down, he has a very good heart."

Logan chuckled. "Is there anyone you can't find something good in?"

"I hope I never meet a person like that. Even those awful Jones brothers must have a little good inside them."

She snuggled a little closer to her husband. In a few weeks, her sister, Sophia, would arrive. In a few months, their baby would be here as well. Elli's heart felt like it would burst out of her chest from the excitement

"I love you, Sheriff."

"I love you too, Elli."

Elli couldn't think of a better place to be than right here, with this man, in Trace Hollow, Montana.

Epilogue

October 1, 1892 - Trace Hollow, Montana

Dear Miriam (and Leonard),

Our first match could not have been more successful. There are always a few bumps in the road to marital bliss, but Elli and Logan have certainly become close.

We have chosen a groom for Sophia. His name is Ethan and he's tall, as you said she is. He has no family here, so a wife that can cook as well as Elli does would certainly be a good match for him. He's been looking a little thin. Ethan is our town attorney and a good Christian man. He is sometimes a little scatter-minded because he does so many things in his line of work—land deeds, banking items, and he's also been working on a project for the state of Montana. You've told me she is level-headed, with a heart for children, and Elli has nothing but good things to say about her.

CJ Samuels

We can thank Ethan for sending her travel fare so promptly. I wish you could be here for the weddings.

Saralyn and Maddie are our next projects and we continue to pray for their husbands, whomever they shall be.

Love in Christ,
Helen (and Don)

November 5, 1892 - Winchester, Ohio

Elli

Dear Helen (and Don),

Sophia is ready to leave. We miss our girls already, but knowing they are in your hands upon arrival gives us peace of mind. The orphanage will miss her smiling face.

Saralyn will be next. She has brown hair, brown eyes, and is the same height as Elli. She also has a heart for animals. In fact, we've both caught her in church with mice and squirrels in her pockets numerous times while growing up.

Maddie, our final girl to soon turn eighteen, is our petite golden-haired sweetheart. Maddie's a dreamer and finds good in everything and everyone.

We shall share more as their turns come up.

Blessings,

Miriam (and Leonard)

ABOUT THE AUTHOR

CJ Samuels, a born and bred Buckeye fan, was born and raised in rural Ohio. After more than twenty years working in service at an auto dealership, she picked up the proverbial pen and began writing, thanks to a lot of encouragement from her family and friends.

CJ Samuels

CJ always has a pot of coffee on and a welcoming chair for anyone who needs to talk. CJ was the daughter of the local preacher and has three kids of her own. From an attorney, to finished construction builder, to a Marine – her kids are her pride and joy. CJ has many "adopted" extra family members, including eleven grandchildren that she claims as her own.

CJ also has three rescue dogs—an English bulldog named Sammie, a chi-weenie named Lucy, and a beagle mix named Lucky. In each of her books, you will find stories from her family history. In her eyes, family is most important.

Contact CJ Samuels on Amazon, Facebook, or at her email cjsamuelsbooks@gmail.com.

Join CJ's Newsletter

158

Also by CJ Samuels

Coming Soon

169

Mail Order Brides of Trace Hollow
Book Two
She knew she would face hardships...
she didn't think being alone
would be one of them.
Sophia
CJ Samuels
Bestselling Author